THE CAT WHO SMELLED A RAT

ALSO BY LILIAN JACKSON BRAUN

THE CAT WHO COULD READ BACKWARDS
THE CAT WHO ATE DANISH MODERN
THE CAT WHO TURNED ON AND OFF
THE CAT WHO SAW RED
THE CAT WHO PLAYED BRAHMS
THE CAT WHO PLAYED POST OFFICE
THE CAT WHO KNEW SHAKESPEARE
THE CAT WHO SNIFFED GLUE
THE CAT WHO WENT UNDERGROUND
THE CAT WHO TALKED TO GHOSTS
THE CAT WHO LIVED HIGH
THE CAT WHO KNEW A CARDINAL
THE CAT WHO MOVED A MOUNTAIN
THE CAT WHO WASN'T THERE
THE CAT WHO WENT INTO THE CLOSET
THE CAT WHO CAME TO BREAKFAST
THE CAT WHO BLEW THE WHISTLE
THE CAT WHO SAID CHEESE
THE CAT WHO TAILED A THIEF
THE CAT WHO SANG FOR THE BIRDS
THE CAT WHO SAW STARS
THE CAT WHO ROBBED A BANK

THE CAT WHO HAD 14 TALES
(SHORT-STORY COLLECTION)

LILIAN JACKSON BRAUN

THE

CAT

WHO

SMELLED

A RAT

BOOKSPAN LARGE PRINT EDITION

G. P. PUTNAM'S SONS NEW YORK

This Large Print Edition, prepared especially for Bookspan, contains the complete, unabridged text of the original Publisher's Edition.

G. P. Putnam's Sons
Publishers Since 1838
a member of
Penguin Putnam Inc.
375 Hudson Street
New York, NY 10014

ISBN 0-7394-1409-7
Printed in the United States of America

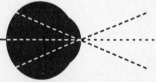

This Large Print Book carries the Seal of Approval of N.A.V.H.

Dedicated to Earl Bettinger,
The Husband Who . . .

THE CAT WHO SMELLED A RAT

one

It was late October, and Moose County, 400 miles north of everywhere, was in danger of being wiped off the map. In the grip of a record-breaking drought, towns and farms and forests could be reduced to ashes overnight—given a single spark and a high wind. Volunteer firefighters were on round-the-clock alert, and the congregations of fourteen churches prayed for snow. Not rain. Snow! Winter always began with a three-day blizzard, called the Big One, that buried everything under snow drifting to ten feet. So the good folk of Moose County waxed their snow shovels, bought antifreeze and earmuffs, stockpiled bottled water and flashlight batteries—and prayed.

Late one evening, in a condominium northeast of Pickax City, the county seat, a cat sat on a windowsill, stretching his neck, raising his nose, and sniffing. The man watching him thought, He smells a skunk. They had recently moved to the wooded area with its new sights, new sounds, new smells.

He went outdoors to investigate and found no sign of a skunk. It was a calm, quiet night—until the whoop of a police siren shattered the silence, followed by the honk-honk of a fire truck speeding south on a distant highway. The noise stopped abruptly as the emergency vehicles reached their destination. Reassured that another wildfire was under control, he went back indoors.

The cat was lapping water from his bowl. It was remarkable that he had smelled smoke three miles away, on a night without a breeze, and with the window closed. But Kao K'o Kung was a remarkable cat! They had moved to a condominium in Indian Village for the winter: two Siamese and their personal valet, Jim Qwilleran. He also wrote a twice-weekly column for the local paper, the *Moose County Something*. Now middle-aged, he had been a prize-winning crime reporter for metropolitan newspapers Down Below, as the rest of the United States was known to Moose County. Odd circumstances had brought him to the north country with his two housemates, both adopted after crises in their nine lives.

Kao K'o Kung, familiarly known as Koko, was a sleek, stalwart male with amazing intelligence and intuition. Yum Yum was smaller, softer, and sweeter. Both had the pale fawn fur with seal brown "points" typical of the breed, and their brown masks were accented with shockingly blue eyes. While the female was adored for her dainty walk and kittenish ways, the male was admired for his masterful whiskers—sixty instead of the usual forty-eight.

By coincidence, Qwilleran was noted for his luxuriant pepper-and-salt moustache. It appeared at the head of his "Qwill Pen" column every Tuesday and Friday and was recognized everywhere he went. A well-built six-foot-two, he was seen walking around town, riding a bicycle, dining in restaurants, and covering his beat. But he had claims to fame other than the unorthodox spelling of his name and the magnificence of his moustache. Fate had made him the heir to the vast Klingenschoen fortune, and he was the richest man in the northeast central United States. Turning his wealth over to a foundation for philanthropic purposes had helped to endear him to the citizens of Moose County.

After the smoke-sniffing episode, Qwilleran gave the Siamese their bedtime treat and conducted them to their comfortable room on the balcony, turning on their TV without the sound, to lull them to sleep. Then he sprawled in a large chair and read news magazines until it was time for the midnight news on WPKX: "A brushfire on Chipmunk Road near the Big B minesite has been extinguished by volunteer firefighters from Kennebeck. When they arrived on the scene, the flames were creeping toward the shafthouse, one of ten in the county recently designated as historic places. 'Motorists driving on country roads are once more reminded not to toss cigarettes out the car window,' said a spokesman for the sheriff's department. 'Roadside weeds and forest underbrush are dry as tinder.' This is the third such fire in a week."

Qwilleran tamped his moustache, as he often did when harboring suspicions; strangely, it seemed to be the source of his hunches. He thought, Arson for purposes of vandalism is on the increase nationwide. In Moose County any black-hearted arsonist who wanted to infuriate the populace could torch a shafthouse. Yet locals were reluctant to admit that "it can happen here." Nevertheless, he had been glad to desert the centers of overpopulation, crime, traffic jams and pollution—and accept the quirks of small-town living. He himself was not inclined to gossip, but he was willing to listen to the neighborly exchange of information that flourished in coffee shops, on street corners and through the Pickax grapevine.

At Toodle's Market the next day, where he bought groceries, the three brushfires were the chief topic of conversation. Everyone had a theory. No one believed the sheriff. It was a cover-up. The authorities were trying to avert panic. The groceries were for Polly Duncan, director of the public library. Qwilleran had an arrangement with her. He shopped for her groceries while she slaved in the work place. Then she invited him to dinner. It was more than a practical proposition; Polly was the chief woman in his life—charming, intelligent, and his own age.

The dinner deal was especially convenient in the winter, when he closed his summer place—a converted apple barn—and moved his household to Indian Village. There he owned a condo, a few doors from Polly's. He liked a periodic change of address; it satisfied the wanderlust that had made him a successful journalist Down Below.

Indian Village was an upscale residential development in Suffix Township (which had been annexed by Pickax City after years of wrangling). It extended along the west bank of the Ittibittiwassee River. Rustic cedar-sided buildings were scattered among the trees: condominiums in clusters of four, multiplex apartments, a clubhouse, and a gatehouse. Qwilleran had Unit Four in the cluster called The Willows. Unit Three was occupied by the WPKX meteorologist, Wetherby Goode (real name, Joe Bunker). There was a new neighbor in Unit Two; Kirt Nightingale was a rare-book dealer from Boston, returning to his hometown in middle age. ("What do you suppose is his *real* name?" the village wags whispered.) Polly Duncan, in Unit One, was impressed by his erudition and said, "If we can accept Qwilleran with a QW and a weatherman named Wetherby Goode, we shouldn't flinch at a Nightingale. And he's going to be a nice quiet neighbor."

That was important. The walls of the contiguous units were thin, and there were other construction details that were flawed. But it was a good address with a wonderful location and many amenities for residents.

Arriving at Unit One with bags of groceries, Qwilleran let himself in with his own key (Polly was at the library), greeted her two cats, and refrigerated perishable purchases. All the units had the same layout: a foyer, a two-story living room with a wall of glass overlooking the river, two bedrooms on the balcony, and a kitchen and dining alcove beneath. A garage with space for one vehicle was under the house.

There the similarity ended. Polly's unit was furnished—even overfurnished—with antiques inherited from her in-laws. Qwilleran preferred the stark simplicity of contemporary design, with two or three antique objects for decorative accent. When friends asked, "Why don't you and Polly get married?" he would reply, "Our cats are incompatible." The truth was that he would find it suffocating to live with the appurtenances of the nineteenth century. Polly felt the same way about "modern." They stayed single.

Before leaving, Qwilleran said a few friendly words to Brutus, a muscular, well-fed Siamese, and looked about for Catta, who was younger and smaller. A flicker of movement overhead revealed her perched on a drapery rod. She had the Siamese taste for heights.

"Are you guys all set for the Big One?" he asked. "It won't be long before snow flies!"

There was no answer, but he could read their minds. They sensed that he had cats of his own. They knew he had been there before, even feeding them when *she* was away. But was he to be trusted? What was that large brush on his face?

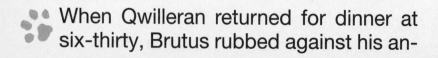 When Qwilleran returned for dinner at six-thirty, Brutus rubbed against his an-

kles; Catta squealed and hopped about. They knew he had a treat in his pocket.

Polly's harried voice came from the kitchen. "Qwill, I'm running a little late. Would you be good enough to feed the cats? Open a can of the Special Diet for him and the salmon in cream gravy for her. . . . And you might put a CD on the stereo. Not Mozart."

"What's for dinner?"

"Minestrone and lasagne."

"How about mandolin music?"

Polly had put a butterfly table and two ladderback chairs in one of the large windows, setting it with Regency silver and Wedgwood.

After adding a plentiful garnish of Parmesan to the soup, Qwilleran asked, "What's the latest news in the stacks?" He knew that the library was the unofficial hub of the Pickax grapevine.

"Everyone's concerned about the brushfires," she said. "The Big B Mine was owned by Maggie Sprenkle's great-grandmother, you know, and if anything happened to the shafthouse, she'd have a heart attack!"

Qwilleran smoothed his moustache. "Has

there ever been a threat to a shafthouse in the past?"

"Not that I know, and I've lived here since college."

"It's ironic that last night's incident should coincide with the dedication of the plaques." Ten bronze plaques, donated anonymously, had been installed at the historic minesites.

"That's exactly what Maggie said. She was the donor, you know, although she doesn't want it known. You won't mention it, will you?"

"Of course not." He had already heard the rumor from three other sources.

When the lasagne was served, conversation turned to the art center's new manager—Barb Ogilvie, the art-knitter.

"A very good choice," Polly said. "She's well organized and has a pleasant personality. She's going to teach a class, and she'll be able to do her own knitting on the job, which will make up for the modest salary they pay. At the craft fair, I bought several pairs of her goofy socks for Christmas gifts."

"Not for me, I hope," Qwilleran said. "By

the way, my compliments on the lasagne. It's one of the best I've ever tasted."

"Thank you. It's from the deli," she said smugly, countering his brash remark about the socks. "Beverly Forfar was never right for the manager's job, although I liked her as a person. I wonder where she is now."

"She found work in a large university town, I happen to know," Qwilleran said. "She won't have to worry about chickens crossing the road, or tractors dumping mud on the pavement."

"She had a strange haircut, didn't she?"

"Yes, but good legs."

"Help yourself to the sauce, Qwill. Mildred made it. The recipe came from the chef at the Mackintosh Inn."

"The local Clan of Mackintosh presented the inn with an antique Scottish curling stone—did you know? It's in a glass case in the lobby," he said. "Is Nightingale still staying at the inn?"

"No, the moving van finally arrived from Boston, with his furniture and books. How could it have taken them so long?"

"They got lost," Qwilleran guessed. "They couldn't find Pickax on the map.

They had a triple load and delivered here by way of Miami and St. Louis."

They had met Kirt Nightingale at a welcoming party in the Village and were impressed by his expertise, although they found him ordinary in appearance and without much personality. He intended to publish his own catalogue and do mail-order business from his condo.

Qwilleran, a collector of old books, had asked a question about Dickens, and the dealer said, "If you're interested, I can get you three volumes of *Sketches by Boz* for thirty thousand. Two were printed in 1836 and the third a year later."

Qwilleran nodded seriously. He never paid more than three or five dollars for a preowned classic at the used-book store in Pickax.

When he and Polly recalled the incident over dinner at the butterfly table, she said, "Don't you think it gives us a certain éclat to have a rare-book dealer in our midst?"

"How much éclat do you want?" he asked. "We already have you and me and the WPKX meteorologist and the publisher of the newspaper and a city council member—and the Indian Village developer himself!" The last one was added with sarcasm; Don Exbridge was not highly admired by the residents. They blamed him for the thin walls, leaking roofs, rattling windows, and bouncing floors. But it was, they told themselves, a good address.

After the dessert—fresh pears and Gorgonzola—Qwilleran built a fire in the fireplace, and they had their beverages in front of the comforting blaze: tea for her, coffee for him. He knew her so well but not well enough to ask, "What kind of coffee do you use? How long has it been in the house? How do you store it? What brewing method do you use?"

She asked, "How's the coffee, dear?" She knew he was a connoisseur.

"Not bad," he replied, meaning it was drinkable.

"I'm glad you like it. It's only instant decaf."

Later, when he was leaving, he noticed a carved wooden box on the foyer table. It was long compared to its other dimensions, and the hinged lid was carved with vines and leaves surrounding the words LOVE BOX.

"Where did you get the box?" he asked.

"Oh, that!" she said with a shrug. "On the day the moving van came, I thought it would be neighborly to invite Kirt in for a simple supper, and the box was a thank-you, I suppose."

She had shortened the man's splendiferous name to a single syllable. "What is its purpose?" he asked crisply.

"It's for gloves. The first letter is half-hidden by the leaves. It had belonged to his mother, and he wanted me to have it. It seemed like a rather touching gesture."

"Hmff," he muttered.

"Actually I don't care for the light oak and stylized carving. It seems rather mannish, and I have a lovely needlepoint glove box that my sister made. . . . I wish you'd take it, Qwill."

"How old is it?"

"Early twentieth century, I'd guess . . . But whatever you do, don't let Kirt know I gave it away! We'll put it in a large plastic bag, in case he's looking out the window when you carry it home."

The glove box looked good on the sleek modern chest of drawers in Qwilleran's foyer—old enough to be interesting but not old enough to look fussy. He immediately filled it with his winter gloves: wool knit, leather, fur-lined. It stood alongside a handmade lamp from the craft exhibit—a tall square column of hammered copper. The Siamese sensed something new and came to investigate. Koko's nose traced the letters on the lid from right to left. "He reads backwards," Qwilleran always said.

Then—abruptly—the cat's attention was distracted. He jumped down from the chest and went to a southeast window, where he stretched his neck, raised his head, and sniffed, while his tail switched nervously.

Without waiting to hear the scream of the police sirens and urgent bleat of the fire truck, Qwilleran ran out to his van just as his neighbor, the weatherman, was returning from his late-evening report.

Qwilleran rolled down the car window. "Joe! Quick! Get in!"

Wetherby Goode was a husky, happy-go-lucky fellow, always ready for an adventure—no questions asked. Settled in the passenger seat, he asked casually, "Where to?"

"I think there's another fire—to the southeast. Open the window and see if you smell smoke."

"Not a whiff . . . but southeast would be across the river. Turn right at the gate and right again at the bridge."

That took them to the intersection of Sprenkle and Quarry roads. They stopped and looked in three directions and sniffed hard. There was no traffic on these back roads at this hour.

"Go east another mile to Old Glory Road," Wetherby said.

"There's a mine down there," Qwilleran said. "Has it occurred to anyone that these fires are at minesites?"

"Well, the theory is that these abandoned mines are bordered by secluded dirt roads that kids use as lovers' lanes. The chances are that they smoke and throw cigarettes out the window. . . . You don't hear of any fires starting in daylight."

Approaching the Old Glory Mine, they could see the taillights of a car receding in the distance.

"See what I mean? I see a red glow just ahead!"

Qwilleran stopped the van and used his cell phone to report a brushfire at Old Glory

Mine. They waited until they heard the emergency vehicles on the way, then drove back to the Village.

"It was my cat who smelled smoke," Qwilleran said. "Koko sees the invisible, hears the inaudible, and smells the unsmellable."

"Jet Stream never smells anything unless it's food," Wetherby said.

"Have you met the new guy in Unit Two?"

"I introduced myself out on the sidewalk one day, and we had a few words. I asked what had happened to the Jaguar he drove when he came here. He said it was too conspicuous among all the vans and pickups, so he disposed of it in Lockmaster and bought a station wagon, four-wheel-drive."

"Has he discovered our dirty little secret?" Qwilleran asked. "If the roof leaks on his thirty-thousand-dollar books, XYZ Enterprises will get sued for plenty."

"The roofs have been fixed!" Wetherby said. "Just in time for the worst drought in twenty years—wouldn't you know? But you were at the beach this summer when they reroofed the whole Village!"

"How come? Did Don Exbridge have a near-death experience?"

"You missed the fun, Qwill. A few of us got together and vandalized the XYZ billboard at the city limits—the one that says, 'We stand behind our product.' A prime example of corporate hogwash! Well, we went out after dark and pasted a twelve-foot patch over it, saying, 'We stand under our roofs with a bucket.' We tipped off the newspaper, of course. The sheriff's night patrol stopped, and the deputy had a good laugh. It didn't hurt that one of the vandals was a city council member. The roofers were on the job the next day!"

Qwilleran said, "That story's good enough for a drink, Joe. Do you have time?"

"Next time, Qwill. I have to get up early tomorrow and drive to Horseradish for a family picnic—last get-together before snow flies. I hear you're driving a limousine in the Shafthouse Motorcade."

"Yes, and I may live to regret it."

two

It was Hixie Rice's idea to stage a Shafthouse Motorcade. She was promotion director for the *Moose County Something,* and the newspaper agreed to underwrite expenses as a public service. Dwight Somers, a public relations consultant, donated his services, and the third member of the planning committee was Maggie Sprenkle, the "anonymous" donor of the ten bronze plaques.

There were ten abandoned mines in Moose County, some dating as far back as 1850. Mining and lumbering had made it the richest county in the state before World War One. Now the minesites were expanses of barren ground enclosed in high chain-link fences and posted with red signs saying: DANGER—KEEP OUT. In the center of each site was the old shafthouse—a weathered wood tower about forty feet high. Architecturally, it looked like a lofty pile of sheds on top of sheds.

A tourist magazine had called it "a cubist artwork—so ugly, it's beautiful!"

Artists painted impressions of the shafthouses in watercolors and oils. Visitors' cameras clicked thousands of times—no, tens of thousands! Locals revered the shafthouses as monuments to the county's distinguished past.

On the morning of the motorcade, while Qwilleran was preparing a particularly toothsome breakfast for the Siamese, he tuned in the hourly news briefs on WPKX and heard:

"Another wildfire in the vicinity of a minesite was reported during the night and brought under control by Kennebeck firefighters. The Old Glory Mine in Suffix Township was the scene of burning weeds and underbrush, threatening the shafthouse, one of the oldest in the county.

All ten shafthouses will be honored as historic places this afternoon when the Shafthouse Motorcade winds through the back roads, dedicating the newly installed bronze markers. County commissioners will officiate."

Without waiting for the high school football scores, he turned the radio off. Then the doorbell rang, and the most glamorous young woman in town was standing on the doorstep. "I got your message. I'm on my way to work. What's the problem?"

Fran Brodie, a resident of Indian Village, was second in command at Amanda's Studio of Interior Design. She was also the police chief's daughter—a fact that counted for something in Qwilleran's book.

"Come in and look around," he said. "This place has been in mothballs all summer and looks neglected. . . . Cup of coffee?"

She accepted and walked around with it, studying the interior. "After snow flies," she said, "the view from these windows will be all black and white. You could use a splash of red over the mantel, and I have a batik wall hanging, three-by-four, done by a new artist in town." Noting the vacant look on her client's face, she added, "As you probably know, that's painting on fabric, using a wax-and-dye method, centuries old. We'll repeat the red in some polished cotton toss pillows for the sofa—large plump ones. The cats will love them! And I'll send you a bowl of red delicious apples for the coffee table. Don't try to eat them; they're painted wood." She had a breezy manner with her male clients that intimidated some and entertained others. Qwilleran was always amused.

She went on. "Where did you get that copper lamp? Not from me! The shade is all wrong."

It was the tall lamp on the chest in the foyer. "Don't you like it? A local metalsmith had it in the craft show."

"It's all right, but it would look a hundred percent better with a brown shade—a square pyramidal shape to complement the square base. I'll send one over with the batik and pillows."

"And wooden apples," Qwilleran reminded her.

"Who scattered the seating pieces like this?"

"Probably the painters when they repaired the water damage."

"My installer will arrange it properly when he makes the deliveries. I'll have him group it in a U-plan, facing the fireplace. Then all you need is an important rug." Her well-made-up face that had been frowning in concentration suddenly brightened. "I know where you can get a lush Danish rya rug—handmade—six-by-eight—vintage design, circa 1950—"

"For only ten thousand," he said with a smirk.

Fran gave him a brief look of annoyance. "It's in the silent auction tomorrow. You'll have to bid on it. It's a vetted sale, and I was on the selection committee. That's how I know about it."

"Should I know what a silent auction is?"

"Well, the way this one works . . . business firms and individuals have donated items to be sold, proceeds going to the Pickax animal shelter. They'll be on display at the community hall. You buy an admission ticket, walk around and look at them, drink some punch, enjoy the entertainment, and socialize. If you see an item you like, you sign your name and the amount you want to bid. Someone else can come along and raise your bid. That's what makes it exciting."

"Hmmm," Qwilleran mused. "How much do you think I should bid on the rug—that is, if I like it."

"The minimum acceptable bid is five hundred. You can take it from there. It's fun to go around and see who's bidding on what—and how much. Friends raise each other's bids—just for deviltry."

"Arch Riker might like to attend," Qwilleran said with malice aforethought.

"I hope you get the rug," Fran said. "The cats will love it!" On the way out she saw the carved oak glove box alongside the copper lamp. "Is that where you store your old love letters?"

Qwilleran immediately phoned the Riker residence. Arch had been his lifelong friend, and now he was editor in chief and publisher of the *Something;* his wife, Mildred, was food editor.

She answered.

"What's Arch doing?" Qwilleran demanded.

"Reading out-of-town newspapers."

"Put him on."

His friend came to the phone with the preoccupied attitude of one who is three days behind with his *New York Times*.

"Arch!" Qwilleran shouted to get his attention. "How would it be if the four of us went to Sunday brunch at Tipsy's Tavern tomorrow? And then to the silent auction at the community hall? I hear they have some pretty good stuff."

It was an irresistible invitation to a gourmand who was also a collector. "What time? Who drives? Do they take credit cards?" Arch asked.

Pleased with the arrangements, Qwilleran dressed for the motorcade and went downtown for an early lunch. Whatever time he had to kill before the push-off could be spent enjoyably at the used-book store. He had his favorite Reuben sandwich at Rennie's in the Mackintosh Inn and was about to leave the building when he heard his name called.

"Qwill! I was just thinking about you!"

"Think of the devil . . . How's everything with you, Barry?"

"Great!"

The K Fund, now owners of the inn, had

sent Barry Morghan from Chicago to manage it.

"Are you ready for the Big One?" Qwilleran asked.

"As ready as I'll ever be. It can't be as bad as they say."

"All that—and worse. But if you can survive the first three days, you're home free. The county has a fleet of snow-handling equipment comparable to a Greek shipping magnate's fleet of oil tankers—thanks to the K Fund."

"Great! Do you have a couple of minutes to talk?"

They stepped into a reading alcove in a secluded corner of the lobby, close by the full-length lifesize portrait of Anne Mackintosh Qwilleran.

"What's on your mind?" Qwilleran asked.

"My brother and his wife are here. They wanted to get settled before snow flies. . . . Listen to me! I'm beginning to talk like a native!"

"Where are they living?"

"They bought one of those big old houses on Pleasant Street. Fran Brodie is fixing it up for them. And the clinic is almost ready to open: Moose County Dermatology, it's called. My sister-in-law is an artist, you know. She does batik wall hangings, and Fran is representing her."

"Interesting!" Qwilleran said. "Is there anything I can do to welcome them?"

"Well, yes," Barry said. "When I first came here, you gave me some great advice about getting along with folks in a small town, and I'd appreciate it if you'd repeat it."

"Be happy to."

"If we could get together at my apartment for dinner some evening, Chef Wingo would cater it, and we'd have more privacy than in a restaurant."

"Great!" Qwilleran said.

It was still too early to report to the courthouse, so he strolled to the used-book store. It was located behind the post office—on a back street that the city's founding fathers, in their wisdom, had named Back Street. It was hardly more than an alley and only a block long, being dead-ended at north and south by busy thoroughfares. In the middle of the block huddled a stone edifice resembling a grotto, built of feldspar that sparkled in the sunlight. No wonder it was Number One on every tourist's sightseeing list. It was originally a smithy, but the blacksmith's grandson had operated it as a used-book store for more than fifty years, and to celebrate its golden jubilee the city of Pickax renamed the block Book Alley.

Edd's Editions, it was called. Entering the shop and blinking to adjust from exterior sunshine to interior gloom, Qwilleran stood still and inhaled the familiar aroma of old books from damp basements, clam chowder being heated for the bookseller's lunch, and leftover sardines in the cat's dish. A large dust-colored longhair patrolled the premises, dusting the books with his plumed tail. He knew Qwilleran.

"Good morning, Winston," he said. "I bet I know what you had for breakfast!"

Eddington Smith heard the voice and came from the back room, where he had his bookbinding equipment and living quarters. Qwilleran had been back there when he was writing a column on bookbinding, and he remembered the man's narrow cot, the cracked mirror over the washbowl, old-fashioned shaving tackle, a two-burner gas stove, a large box of matches—and a small handgun.

Eddington had a slight build that was shrinking with age. His hair was gray; his skin had a gray pallor; and his drab clothing blended in with the gray covers of old books that were stacked on tables, shelves, and floor.

"My best customer!" he said when he had adjusted his glasses and recognized Qwilleran. "I've found something special for you!" He hurried back into the inner sanctum.

There was another customer in the store—a stranger with a flashlight, risking his life on the rickety wooden stepladder. Qwilleran thought, He's a book scout, hunting for buried treasure.

When Eddington returned, he was clutching a large-format book to his chest. "You're interested in Egypt, Mr. Q. Here's a beautiful volume—not terribly old, good condition, scholarly text, well illustrated. *Mysteries of the Egyptian Pyramids*."

Qwilleran glanced at the stepladder; the stranger was listening. He was looking for a book he could buy for three dollars and sell to an antiquarian bookseller for fifteen, after which it would go into the catalogue for two hundred—or two thousand.

"I'll take it, sight unseen," Qwilleran said. "How much?"

"How about twenty-five cents?" Edd said with a twinkle in his eye; he had playful moods.

The stranger dropped his flashlight.

"Isn't that a little high, Edd?" Qwilleran was playing the game. "I'll give you twenty cents," he said. He slipped twenty-five dollars into the bookseller's hand.

"You're my best customer," Eddington said. "I'm leaving my store to you in my will." He always said that.

"Does the bequest include Winston?" Qwilleran asked. "I'm not sure I could afford to feed him."

They were walking toward the door. Obviously the stranger was still listening.

Eddington said, "He's an old cat and doesn't eat much, but he likes to go out to dinner once in a while—at a good restaurant." Edd had never been in such a giddy mood.

Qwilleran took the handsome book, gave Edd the okay sign, and went on his way to another adventure.

* * *

The Shafthouse Motorcade lined up around Park Circle in front of the courthouse: a sheriff's car, three limousines for dignitaries, an airport rental vehicle for the TV crew from Down Below, three cars for news photographers, and a florist's van.

Qwilleran, Hixie Rice, and Dwight Somers would be chauffeuring the limousines borrowed from the local funeral home. Their distinguished passengers would include three county commissioners, the president of the historical society, the county historian and his wife, five direct descendants of the original mine owners, and a fairly large dog.

The five direct descendants were Maggie Sprenkle, the rich widow; the elderly Jess Povey, who called himself a gentleman farmer, although Maggie said he was no gentleman; Amanda Goodwinter, businesswoman and council member; Leslie Bates Harding, age six; and Burgess Campbell, a lecturer on American history at the college. Blind from birth, he was always accompanied by his guide dog, and both were well known in Pickax—Burgess for his sense of humor, and Alexander for his good manners. On this occasion the proud Scot was wearing Highland dress: kilt, sporran, shoulder plaid, and glengarry bonnet.

"Burgess, you look splendid!" Qwilleran complimented him.

"So do you," he quipped.

There was confusion about who would ride with whom. Maggie refused to ride in the same limousine with Jess Povey. Leslie wanted to ride with the dog. Amanda shouted above the hubbub, "I don't care if I ride on the hood! Let's get this show on the road!"

It was decided that Qwilleran's passengers would be Maggie, Leslie, and the ninety-eight-year-old historian Homer Tibbitt, with his wife.

Leslie's mother straightened his tie and combed his hair, saying, "You'll have your picture taken, and it'll be in the newspaper! Grandma will be so proud of you! I'll be here to pick you up when it's over. You'll be riding with that nice man with the big moustache, and he'll take good care of you."

Qwilleran looked askance at the youngster squirming in his little long-pant suit, white shirt, and bow tie. Huffing into his moustache, he said to Maggie, "No one told me I'd have to baby-sit."

She and Leslie took the seat behind the driver, leaving the roomier backseat for the Tibbitts: Homer and his attentive wife, Rhoda. She had brought pillows to make a nest for his bony frame. Leslie, who had never seen anyone so old, knelt on the seat and rode backwards, staring at the furrowed, fretful face.

After a while he pointed a finger at the old gentleman, pulled an imaginary trigger and said, "*Ping!*"

Maggie said, "Turn around and sit down, Leslie, and fasten your seatbelt. We're going to start moving."

The signal was given, and the motorcade pulled away from the courthouse and proceeded up Main Street, where shoppers stood on the curbs and cheered. This was an important event for Moose County. For the next four hours the vehicles zigzagged through the countryside, past the ten minesites on back roads and lightly traveled highways.

The first destination was the Big B Mine that had been owned and operated by Maggie's great-grandmother. When the motorcade stopped, all the car doors opened simultaneously, and the passengers piled out, gathering around the bronze marker. Like all the mines, it was now only an expanse of barren ground, fenced and posted with warnings, the only relic being a weathered wood tower about forty feet high. There was something mysterious, even scary, about the silent, lonely shafthouses.

Maggie and the chief commissioner were posed with the bronze plaque, and a young woman from the florist's van came running with a large wreath tied with purple ribbon, to hang on the post supporting the marker. Photographers jockeyed for angles that would include the shafthouse in the background.

Then the commissioner made his speech about Moose County's proud mining heritage. . . . The thousands of miners and their families who had lived and died here . . . the disasters they endured: cave-ins, explosions, riots . . . their primitive villages of huts, a one-room schoolhouse, a chapel, and a company store. Now there was nothing left but the shafthouse!

He talked a little too long, and the celebrators were glad to return to their cars.

Qwilleran thought, One down and only nine to go!

At the next mine, associated with the Harding family, there were more photographs, another wreath, and another speech by another politician, who said, "Other parts of the country have Niagara Falls, the Grand Canyon, or the Statue of Liberty. We have ten shafthouses!"

A photographer told a direct descendant to take his thumb out of his mouth and try to smile, but Leslie only cocked his finger at the man and said, "*Ping!*"

The rest of the afternoon was reported by Qwilleran himself in his personal journal:

After the first five stops, all the direct descendants had been photographed and had lost interest in the proceedings, but they were trapped. So were the other dignitaries. Photographers from the *Bixby Bugle* and *Lockmaster Ledger* had all the stuff they could use, and they left. The TV crew drove back to the airport after shooting what they considered most newsworthy: Amanda with her built-in scowl and scarecrow style of dressing, and Burgess with his kilt and Alexander.

The speeches were getting shorter—and the listeners fewer. Homer Tibbitt refused to leave the limousine anymore, and Leslie continued to torment him, cocking his finger and saying, "*Ping!*"

"Kid, if you do that one more time," Homer screeched in his high-pitched voice, "I'll bash you with my crutch!"

His wife said, "Leslie, dear, he doesn't have a crutch. Why don't you sit up front with the driver, and you can shoot sheep and cows through the windshield."

"Thank you, Rhoda," I said sotto voce. "You're a sweetheart!"

So Leslie rode with me in the front seat, and I guess I unnerved him by saying, "What kind of ammunition do you use? Do you have a license to carry a handgun? How long have you belonged to the NRA?"

After a while he pounded my arm

and whispered something. "What?" He whispered again. There we were— in the middle of nowhere—surrounded by acres of stony pasture with not a bush in sight! So I leaned on the horn and brought the motorcade to a stop. I checked with the deputy; wasn't there a crossroads store nearby? He said yes—at the next intersection.

When we got there, I grabbed Leslie by the wrist and virtually dragged him into the store. The storekeeper was a character with a beard about a foot long. I said to him, "This young man wishes to use your restroom."

"It ain't a public toilet," he said.

I didn't say a word, but dragged Leslie out to the sheriff's car. A few seconds later a deputy with a service gun in his holster conducted the boy back into the store.

Meanwhile, one of the politicians riding with Dwight went into the store and bought a pint of something. By the time we arrived at our tenth minesite, the pols were stoned, and the direct descendants were bored out of their skulls. Homer was asleep. The photographer had run out of film, and the florist had run out of wreaths.

Such is life in the boondocks!

three

Qwilleran placed his new "old book" from Edd's shop on the coffee table. It had a handsome jacket that had been protected by a plastic slipcover: an illustration of pyramids rising mysteriously from the desert. He thought, Egypt has pyramids; we have shafthouses.

Whenever something new was added, the Siamese had to make an immediate inspection. Yum Yum was subjective in her appraisal. (Can it be batted around? Hidden under a rug? Chewed?) Koko was inclined to be more objective. (What is its purpose? Where did it come from? Why is it here?)

Mysteries of the Egyptian Pyramids came

under close scrutiny. Yum Yum rejected it on all counts; Koko found that it had merit and gave it his blessing: He sat on it. Qwilleran would read aloud from it before leaving for Sunday brunch and the silent auction. They liked the sound of his voice, whether he was reading about ancient Egypt or the World Series. Then, at noon, he gave them a crunchy treat and a few parting instructions: "Drink plenty of water. Take your afternoon naps. Don't make any long-distance phone calls." They listened politely.

Qwilleran picked up Polly and the Rikers in his van. Just in case he bought the six- by eight-foot rug, he wanted to be able to bring it home.

Arch and Mildred were eagerly awaiting an afternoon of food and bargains in the company of their best friends. The couple had found each other late in life, and both had found new careers after retirement. She was plump and pretty and loved to cook; he was paunchy and ruddy-faced and loved to eat.

"Beautiful day!" Mildred said as she climbed into the van.

"It won't be long before snow flies," Polly said.

"It'll put an end to the threat of wildfires," Arch observed.

"Tell them what you've just found out, hon," his wife said.

"Yes. . . It'll be Monday's banner story. A geologist from the state university called and said there's a similar situation in Canada. In abandoned mines it's quite possible that fires have been smoldering underground for as much as a century. Normal rainfall keeps them under control, but they surface as spontaneous conflagrations when drought conditions prevail. All our mines are said to be connected, you know."

"No, I've never heard that," Polly said.

"We should have constant surveillance of the mine area, but the sheriff claims to have insufficient vehicles and personnel for a stepped-up patrol. That's the bad news. The good news comes from Moose County Community College. Burgess Campbell's students propose a Citizens' Fire Watch. Volunteers will drive their own vehicles over prescribed routes in three-hour shifts.

They'll use cell phones to report smoke or burning weeds to a hotline."

Mildred was always optimistic. "They won't have any trouble enlisting volunteers. It's a temporary thing—until snow flies—and it's for a good cause. Everyone wants to save the shafthouses."

Arch said, "Tomorrow's paper will be a fat issue: the wildfire emergency, the motorcade, the silent auction . . . How was the motorcade, Qwill?"

"Interesting," he said.

Tipsy's Tavern in nearby Kennebeck was a roadhouse in a sprawling log cabin that had been noted for good food since the 1930s. The founder had named it after his cat, a white one with comical black markings, and her portrait hung in the main dining room. At one time there had been a countywide controversy over her feet in the painting; should they be black or white? Customers were in complete agreement about the steak and fish, however. It was the best!

The Sunday brunch was a recent innovation, offering "anything you want, as long as it's eggs." They were "laid this morning by happy hens in our own backyard." The yolks were domed and intensely orange-yellow—a good sign, according to Mildred. The house specialty was called Eggs Tipsy. A large English muffin was split and grilled; then each half was topped with a home-made sausage patty, a poached egg, and melted cheddar cheese. Local grandmothers waited on tables.

At Qwilleran's table they entertained themselves by bandying superlatives:

"Tipsy's is the oldest restaurant in the county."

"The Mackintosh Room at the inn is the newest—and best."

"Lois's Luncheonette is the shabbiest and friendliest."

"Otto's Tasty Eats—until it closed—took top honors for being the worst and the noisiest—"

"And probably made the most money. Otto has the building up for sale."

"There's a rumor it's going to be an antique village—a cooperative where dealers rent spaces and take turns minding the store."

Qwilleran knew his guests liked a Bloody Mary before brunch, and he ordered four.

"But make mine without the vodka," he said. "I'm underage."

"Yes, sonny," said the white-haired waitress.

When drinks were served, Arch proposed a toast to Lenny Inchpot, who had won "the last bike race before snow flies."

"His mother will be thrilled," Polly said.

"Lois will be serving free coffee tomorrow. Lenny's a good kid. Ambitious. Hardworking. Conscientious."

Mildred, the only Moose County native in the foursome, said, "He doesn't take after his father. Mr. Inchpot never did a day's work in his life. He was always ill, Lois said. She looked after him, raised their son, and supported them by running the lunchroom. And by the way, her husband drank a little, saying it was good for his condition. One day he came out of a bar, stepped in front of a truck and was killed. Lois went all to pieces—until she found out the truth. Dr. Goodwinter didn't tell her, but his nurse did. There'd never been anything wrong with Mr. Inchpot. He was a malingerer."

Arch said, "That should lay to rest the notion that all the bad guys are in large cities, and all the good guys are in small towns. And how about the forgery ring, Millie?"

"That was way back when I started teaching. Three all-A students were signing report cards, writing absence excuses, and doing the other kids' homework."

The two men exchanged glances. They had grown up together in Chicago. Qwilleran said, "The only time we got into trouble, it was for humorous pranks."

"Like putting glue on the teacher's chair cushion," Arch added.

"Cute!" said Mildred.

They ordered Eggs Tipsy all around, and the plates arrived in about two minutes.

"What took you so long?" Arch asked.

"Gotta wait for the hens to lay the eggs," the white-haired waitress said.

The freshness of the eggs, flavor of the sausage, crispness of the grilled muffins, and zippiness of the cheese were duly noted. Then conversation turned to the haiku contest being sponsored by Qwilleran's column. His readers were invited to compose poems inspired by the Japanese style, mailing them on postal cards to the

Something. Winners would have the thrill of seeing their entries printed on page two, and each would receive a fat yellow lead pencil stamped with "Qwill Pen" in gold.

Arch said, "Our mailroom is swamped! The response is double that of last year. That's amazing, considering we don't offer a two-week vacation in Hawaii or a year's supply of chocolate-coated potato chips."

Qwilleran said, "People of all ages and walks of life like haiku, because the form is written in plain language, about common experiences and emotions, and sometimes with a whimsical slant. An early Japanese poet wrote: *Don't worry, spider; my housekeeping is casual.* And one of last year's winners wrote: *I never know what to say when I speak to a butterfly.*"

He had promised that the winning haiku would be printed "before snow flies."

"You didn't give them much time to create masterpieces," Mildred remarked.

"The shorter the deadline, the more response we get. Give them a month to think, and they forget all about it. What's new at the art center, Mildred?"

"There's an interesting new artist in town.

Her husband is the new dermatologist from Chicago. She's joined the art center. She specializes in batik wallhangings."

"What are those?" Arch asked.

"It's a centuries-old method of painting on fabric, using wax and dye," Qwilleran informed him, enjoying his one-upmanship.

"How do you know?"

"I get around. I'm having dinner with her and the doctor Tuesday night. They want some advice on adjusting to the small-town culture."

"How'd you like to write an advice column for the *Something*?" Arch came back. "You could call it *Q Tips*."

They skipped the bread pudding, and there was no lingering over coffee; their minds were on the auction. It was being staged at the community hall. Not only was the parking lot filled, but the police were allowing cars to park on both sides of Main Street.

At the entrance an older woman greeted Qwilleran with an exuberant hug and shook hands with his guests. She was Maggie Sprenkle, the same rich widow who had donated the bronze plaques, who served loyally on the library board, and who spent long hours at the animal shelter as a volunteer.

Many of those in attendance had bought tickets to support a good cause and spent their time circling the refreshment table in the center of the hall or making friends with the puppies and kittens waiting to be adopted, yipping and mewing, extending paws through the bars of their cages. Serious auction-goers headed for the bidding tables, where antiques, decorative objects, and hand-crafted items were on display.

There were rows of folding chairs here and there, where guests would sit and sip punch. Maggie, a gracious hostess, would ask them, "How do you like the punch? I made it myself. . . . Are you doing any bidding? Keep an eye on the bidding sheets, and don't let anyone top you. . . . Every item is worth at least twice the minimum bid."

Qwilleran perused the offerings quickly until he found the Danish rya rug, draped over a rack and spread out over a table. The bidding sheet said "Minimum bid, $500; Minimum raise, $50." No names had been signed to the sheet; no bids had been made. He signed for five hundred.

The Rikers came along and Arch said in surprise, "Are you bidding on *that*?"

A check of the bidding sheets indicated that Polly was bidding on a pair of Italian porcelain parrots.

Arch, who considered himself a serious and knowledgeable collector, was bidding on a piece of rusty tin.

Qwilleran said to him, "Are you bidding on *that*?"

"It's a fabulous piece of folk art in painted tin," he was informed. "It's a matchbox. The idea is that the cat scares the mice away from the matches."

Guarding the matchbox was the head of a cat with large, rapacious eyes; its tail formed a hook for hanging on a wall.

"What are they bidding on this?" Qwilleran asked.

"It's up to two-fifty. I am willing to go three."

"Three *hundred*?"

"Even at that it's a steal!" A connoisseur of old painted tin, Arch had built an enviable collection Down Below, only to lose it in a divorce settlement. His ex-wife then had the effrontery to open an antique shop and name it Tin 'n' Stuff.

Qwilleran said, "Nice piece of tin. Hope you get it."

He himself went back to the Danish rug to check the bidding. There was not a single name on the sheet, other than his own. Chuckling to himself, he raised his own bid and signed Ronald Frobnitz. Then he went in search of Polly.

"How's it going?" he asked.

"They're pushing the prices too high. I'm dropping out. How about you, Qwill?"

"Someone else is bidding on the rug that Fran Brodie wanted me to have, but I'm keeping my eye on it."

The crowd was moving toward the stage at the end of the hall, and he rounded up his party for a show featuring professional canines and their handlers.

First there was a German shepherd from the Moose County sheriff's department, trained for search and rescue. He had found lost children, missing persons, fugitives, and accident victims. He listened modestly as his handler extolled his intelligence and perseverance. "He—never—gives—up!"

From Bixby County came a black Labrador retriever trained for drug searching. She amused the audience by retrieving a folded towel again and again with unflagging enthusiasm. Her handler said, "In training sessions, narcotics of different kinds are wrapped in the towel. In a drug raid she can spot nine kinds of contraband."

The audience waited expectantly for another extraordinary dog, when who should amble on stage but the six-foot-eight Derek Cuttlebrink with his guitar. The audience screamed and applauded. After strumming a few chords with a bouncy rhythm, Moose County's favorite young-man-about-town sang with a nasal twang:

I found my puppy in Pickax
At the animal shelter one day.
* I was feeling down*
* When I come to town,*
And I took him home to stay.
He was jest a li'l white puppy
With a black spot round his eye,
* But he bumbled and he yipped,*
* And he nuzzled and he nipped,*
And he kissed my blues goodbye.

"Sing it again!" everyone yelled.

He strummed a few chords. "Everybody sing!"

Loudly, and unsure of the lyrics, they sang, "I found my puppy in Pickax . . . da-duh, da-da-da da da da da . . ."

Polly groaned.

"They like it," Qwilleran said.

"It's the kind of inane jingle that haunts one. I'll have to hum the *Hallelujah Chorus* to get it out of my mind."

Derek loped off the stage with the lazy, long-legged gait that his groupies adored.

"You know, Qwill, Maggie Sprenkle commissioned him to write it for the occasion, but he wouldn't take money for it."

"And rightly so," Qwilleran said as he looked at his watch. "Excuse me while I check the bidding." No one but him and the fictitious Ronald Frobnitz had placed a bid on the Danish rug. He raised the bid to a thousand under his own name, telling himself it was a good cause. Then he checked the porcelain parrots. Bidders had been active. A minute before the deadline, he raised the bid under his name.

A bell rang, and bidders flocked to the display tables. There were groans of disappointment and cries of success. He wrote checks for the rug and the parrots and presented the latter to Polly. "This is your Christmas gift."

"You've already given me my Christmas gift," she protested, showing a handsome cameo ring, "and it's only October."

"This is your Christmas gift for next year."

Arch paid for his tin matchbox, and Mildred asked him to write a check for a Chinese porcelain bowl she had bought.

Qwilleran said to Maggie Sprenkle, "I was hoping you'd donate the French crystal pitcher I admired at your house when I was there. I would have bid high on it."

"You have good taste, Qwill. That's a St. Louis lead crystal martini pitcher from the steamship *Liberté*. It's documented. Mr. Sprenkle and I crossed the Atlantic many times on the French liners."

The foursome drove back to Indian Village, saying, "Good haul! Lots of laughs! . . . Wasn't Derek a scream! . . . Maggie says a lot of kittens and puppies were adopted." They laid Qwilleran's new rug and said, "Not my taste, but gorgeous! . . . Absolutely wild! . . . Why, it's in Siamese colors!"

When the guests had gone, the Siamese emerged from nowhere, cautiously, to confront the wonder that had been added to their world. Yum Yum never walked across an area rug of any size or composition, always taking the long way around to reach her destination, and the new obstacle was six by eight, with deep pile. Even Koko was dubious about the wild tumble of yarns. With ears and whiskers back, he sniffed the edge and put forth a trembling paw to test it—dead or alive? They both jumped when the phone rang. It was the attorney, G. Allen Barter.

"What's up, Bart?" Qwilleran asked briskly. Such a call on a Sunday sounded urgent.

"I just had a call from the hospital. Eddington Smith died this afternoon. Heart attack. He'd had a history of heart trouble, you know. He was able to press the medical-alert button, but they couldn't save him. He was one of our pro bono clients, so they called me. He has no family."

"This is astounding!" Qwilleran said. "I saw him in the store yesterday, and he was in a playful mood, although he never looked healthy. . . . Well, what can I say? A lot of us will miss him. . . . And wait a minute, Bart! What about Winston?"

"We'll find a good home for him."

"Meanwhile, someone should feed him."

"We'll send one of our clerks over."

"He eats only sardines."

"Cynthia knows that. She fed Winston last year while Edd was hospitalized."

Qwilleran said, "I'll write an obit for tomorrow's paper. I probably knew him as well as anyone did."

"Yes, he considered you more of a friend than a customer. You may know that his will makes you heir to the bookstore, building and all."

"What! He used to joke about it, but—"

"It was no joke, but we can talk about that later. Meanwhile, yes—you're the right one to do the obituary."

four

Qwilleran knew what time she would be leaving for work on Monday morning. He waited on his doorstep until her small car backed out of its underground slot, then went to meet her.

She lowered the car window. "Qwill! You can't imagine how perfect the parrots are on my mantel. Beautiful glaze! Wonderful shade of green! And so tasteful! I can't help wondering who donated them."

"I'm curious about the Danish rug. No one in this neck of the woods has any contemporary. Where has it been for the last fifty years? It accomplishes what Fran wanted; it sparks the whole room. She's sending over a few more items with decorative pizzazz."

"Have the cats pronounced their verdict about the rug?" Polly asked.

"The jury is still out. They'll have to deliberate for a couple of days. . . . But on a serious note, Polly, have you heard about Eddington Smith? It was on the air."

"I haven't been listening."

"He died yesterday. Heart attack."

"Oh, that dear man!" Polly said. "He was approaching eighty and was never healthy, but he did all the repairs and bookbinding for the library—in that stuffy back room. We shall miss him."

"I stayed up half the night writing his obituary," Qwilleran said, "and I must admit it's one of my better pieces of funerary prose. Would your board of directors consider a memorial to Eddington—an annual scholarship or essay contest for the lower grades, or both? The K Fund would go fifty-fifty."

"Definitely. I'll call a special meeting tonight."

"Be sure to send a release to the newspaper."

"I will. . . . What are you doing today, Qwill?"

"Just puttering around."

When the black commercial van came slowly down River Road, Yum Yum disappeared, but Koko hopped on and off the windowsill in excitement, as if he knew this was an authorized delivery. The door of the van was tastefully lettered in gold: Amanda's Studio of Interior Design. The driver was a big, blond fellow in a black nylon jacket lettered on the back: MUDVILLE CURLERS.

Qwilleran went out to meet him. "Are you on the curling team in Sawdust City?"

"Yep," said the young man as he started to unload.

"I hear that's quite an interesting sport."

"Yep."

First he brought in the square brown lampshade for the square-based copper lamp. It was obviously ten times better than the former shade, which was round and ivory-colored.

Next came the bowl of shiny red apples and the pair of red pillows for the sofa, followed by a crate of five plant pots filled with red geraniums.

"What are those?" asked the surprised customer.

"Plants. She said to put them up there on the top railing."

"On the balcony?"

"That's what she said."

The pots were placed at intervals of about a foot. Fran always insisted that four are better than three, and five are better than four. She never stated her reasoning; anyone as attractive and talented as Fran needed no reasons.

Finally came the wall hanging, measuring three-by-four. It covered much of the brick chimney breast—a stylized nature study of two red-breasted robins tugging a worm out of a lawn. Everything was superscale: the robins in the foreground as big as turkeys, the green leaves in the background as big as a pizza, and the worm as big as a salami.

After hanging it and checking it with a small level, the installer stood back to survey it. "Cool!" he said to Qwilleran. "They're robins."

"They're big enough to be turkeys," Qwilleran observed.

"Yeah. Artists do crazy things like that."

Qwilleran did his puttering at the office of the *Moose County Something*, when he handed in copy for the obituary. He scanned page proofs, and checked photos and final drafts. There were photos of ten mines and five direct descendants. . . . Coverage on the silent auction included shots of Derek Cuttlebrink and the two G-dogs, as well as a satisfied customer carrying away a rocking chair. . . . Eddington Smith's farewell ran on the obituary page with a photo of the store and a photo-file shot of the late bookseller.

Only Qwilleran knew the story behind the story of the motorcade: the politicians' speeches getting shorter and shorter, dignitaries refusing to leave the limousines, the county historian asleep on a backseat, nine wreaths for ten mines, and a direct descendant taking potshots at everyone with his index finger. *Ping!* And more!

In the column of news briefs on the business page Qwilleran found three items of note:

The Pickax shop of Exbridge & Cobb, Fine Antiques, has achieved the long-time goal of Susan Exbridge: acceptance as an exhibitor at the Eastside Settlement House Antique Show in New York, one of the most prestigious in the country.

Theo Morghan, M.D., and David Todd, M.D., both of Chicago, have arrived here to open the Moose County Dermatology Clinic in the medical center. Specialties are skin diseases, plastic surgery, and liposuction.

Donald Exbridge, CEO of XYZ Enterprises, announces the dissolution of the eight-year-old corporation and the formation of a new enterprise: Donex & Associates. The move coincides with the resignation of two principals: Henry Zoller is retiring, and Caspar Young will establish his own construction business. The flagship development of XYZ, Indian Village, will continue under the management of Donex.

The new Pet Plaza in Kennebeck is booked to capacity for October. According to a spokesperson, it is "designed for pet owners who feel guilty about leaving their loved ones in a boarding kennel while they take luxury cruises.'' Reservations are being accepted for November.

Qwilleran enjoyed a few chuckles over the news briefs. They had been slyly edited with Don Exbridge's ex-wife as the lead item, while Don's new firm was sandwiched between skin diseases and animal hospitality. Had the billboard prank caused the upheaval? Who were the unnamed associates?

It was a good excuse to visit Susan Exbridge's shop on Main Street.

''Darling! How wonderful to see you!'' she exclaimed in the dramatic manner she affected. ''Did you come to spend money or scrounge a cup of coffee?''

''The latter. I'm honest to a fault. . . . Also I want to congratulate you on making the New York show. Your late partner would be proud of you.''

''Thank you. The show is too grand for words.''

He followed her to the office, through an aisle of polished mahogany and brass.

"Do you want your coffee black?"

"Please . . . There was another interesting item on the business page today. What do you suppose Donex & Associates have up their corporate sleeve?"

"Nothing entirely honorable, I'm sure."

Qwilleran said, "I've never met the Y and Z part of the firm."

"They're well rid of the connection, if you ask me. Cass Young is a nice young man; Dr. Zoller is a nice older man. He gave up his dental practice because he couldn't bear to hurt his patients. Besides, he was better at playing the stock market than filling teeth, and he had family money to play with. . . . Is it true that you've moved to the Village for the winter? You and Polly must attend the rally in the clubhouse—to support Amanda's candidacy, you know. Bring that new neighbor of yours. I'd like to meet a rare-book dealer. What's his name?"

"Kirtwell Nightingale."

"I like him already. I have a new neighbor, too—an older woman from Baltimore, recently retired. She has some fabulous eighteenth-century Americana that I'd like to buy."

"What is she doing 400 miles north of everywhere?" Qwilleran inquired.

"She lost her husband, and her son thought she should come here."

Qwilleran said, "I hope she likes snow-shoeing and ice fishing. What did she do before she retired?"

"Accounting, but her hobby is astrology—serious astrology. She's highly regarded on the East Coast, according to her son, and I'd like to see her get established here. She's giving a lecture at the clubhouse, and I've commissioned her to do my natal chart."

Qwilleran thought, The woman probably owns a priceless Hepplewhite sideboard that Susan wants to take to the New York show.

Susan suggested, "Why don't you have Mrs. Young do your chart, Qwill?"

"You mean, my horoscope?"

"I'm not talking about the silly things your paper prints to fill space on the comic page, darling! Simply provide the place, date, and hour of your birth, and Mrs. Young will chart the effect of the planets on your past, present, and future."

Qwilleran huffed into his moustache. He knew his past and present and preferred not to know his future. On impulse he asked, "Who's her son?"

"The Y in XYZ Enterprises, but he's going out on his own. Do you happen to know the hour of your birth, Qwill? Not too many persons do."

"Seven minutes after eleven P.M.—a lucky number, my mother said."

"I'd say you were lucky, darling."

"Off and on. Could I have my . . . *chart* done anonymously?"

"You can use an assumed name, and I won't reveal anything about you. That way, the chart will be a demonstration of the integrity of the science—and Mrs. Young's skill."

He wrote down the data required and the name Ronald Frobnitz. "How much is this little charade going to cost?"

"No more than you can afford . . . another cup?"

"No thanks, but it's good! What brand of instant decaf do you buy?"

"Get out!" she screamed.

He started to wander out through the

empty store. "Customers aren't breaking down your doors today."

"It's Monday."

He sauntered past Chippendale, Queen Anne, chinoiserie, then stopped before a framed piece of needlework. The embroidery threads were faded, and the linen was dark with age. Alphabet blocks were stitched to make a border, and in the center was a boy jumping over a lighted candlestick. The inscription read: *Jack be nimble . . . Jack be quick*.

"What's that?" he asked.

"A sampler, late nineteenth century," Susan said. "Not what I usually have in my shop, but it came in a box of quite good engravings."

"I wish I had a buck for every time that nursery rhyme was recited to me. In our house the rule was: Be quick but never in a hurry. The last time I was in a hurry, I was rushing out to play baseball with the kids, and I fell down some concrete steps. Had twelve stitches taken in my upper lip." He patted his moustache.

"Your mother must have been a saint, Qwill, to make a responsible adult out of a brat like you. I'm sure you were a brat."

"Yes, but a decent one. How much for the sampler?"

"Take it!" she said. "I'll never sell it."

On the way home Qwilleran tuned in to WPKX on his car radio to catch the hourly news and heard Derek Cuttlebrink singing in his country western twang, "I found my puppy in Pickax. . . ." That rogue, he thought, has been to the station and taped it, and they'll play it ad nauseam until Christmas! A lot of puppies and kittens might be adopted, but it'll drive the radio audience up the wall!

The broadcast news was merely a condensation of that day's *Moose County Something*, with the exception of a bulletin: "Moose County is in dire crisis! Tune in to WPKX tonight at eight o'clock as civic leaders confront the threat of widespread fire throughout the countryside, forests and small villages. Drastic action is needed! Every citizen should tune in tonight at eight. Alert your friends and neighbors!"

While Qwilleran was downtown, the Siamese were acquainting themselves with the new acquisitions. Returning home he found a corner of the deep-pile rug turned up and two of his yellow pencils hidden underneath—Yum Yum's doing. In the foyer the new shade on the copper lamp had been twisted out of square with the base—Koko's doing. That cat enjoyed rubbing his jaw against the bottom edge of the shades. Otherwise, all was well: The red apples were in their bowl on the coffee table; the red geraniums were lined up on the balcony railing; and the red robins were still tugging at their worm over the fireplace.

Qwilleran said to them, "I've brought something else for you to inspect," and he hung the Jack Be Nimble sampler over a kitchen counter.

The eight o'clock newscast, with all its urgency and disturbing import, was a good excuse for Qwilleran to invite his new neighbor in for a drink, but when he phoned, Nightingale hesitated. "I'm an ailurophobe."

"Have no qualms. The cats will be confined to their quarters on the balcony," Qwilleran assured him. "What do you like to drink?"

"Just a little vodka on the rocks."

In preparation Qwilleran filled two bowls

with mixed nuts and hid the glove box he was not supposed to have. The Siamese were given an extra snack and ushered upstairs.

Kirt Nightingale arrived a quarter-hour before the program was due to start. As he entered, he darted glances into corners and shadows as if expecting to be ambushed. Once reassured, he took a seat on the sofa. Of course, he noticed the book on the coffee table. "Are you interested in Egypt? I can get you *The Journals of Bonaparte in Egypt in 1779 to 1801*. Ten volumes in half-leather. With scientific translations in Arabic."

"Sounds interesting," Qwilleran said, more politely than honestly. "How much?"

"Only seven hundred."

"That's something to think about, definitely."

"Do you know David Roberts?"

It seemed like an abrupt change of subject. Qwilleran knew two men by that name: the sports editor at the paper and the mechanic at Gippel's Garage. Fortunately he had the good sense to ask, "Which one?"

"The eighteenth-century artist who painted Egyptian deserts and architecture.

There are three volumes that you'd appreciate—with more than a hundred hand-
colored lithographs. Published in 1846. The
color is not the original, you understand,
but it's early."

Qwilleran nodded. "Yes, of course.
What's being asked?"

"You could have the three volumes, large
format, for under sixty thousand."

"We'll have to talk about that," Qwilleran
said as he looked at his watch and tuned in
to the eight o'clock program. Music was
abruptly interrupted, heightening the sense
of urgency. Then the station announcer
said, "Tens of thousands of county residents will hear this program and realize the
need for action." He introduced the president of the county commissioners, who had
lauded the shafthouses in flowery terms
and now seemed solemnly concerned: "Dry
conditions, subterranean fires creeping to
the surface, and the chance that high winds
could sweep across the landscape and de-
stroy two hundred square miles of farms,
forests, and towns, converting this fair
county of ours into charcoal overnight! It
happened in the nineteenth century and
could happen again. Routine patrols are not

enough. Our only defense is constant surveillance around the clock. We have fifteen
volunteer fire departments on the alert,
equipped to put down small fires before
they become big fires, but they must know
their location.

"To the rescue comes the Citizens' Fire
Watch, ready to swing into action at midnight. Chairman Ernie Kemple will describe
the operation.

"First let me remind you, folks, that this
idea was proposed by Burgess Campbell's
American history students at MCCC, who
have been working industriously to plan the
operation."

Kemple's booming voice was well
known. Since selling his insurance agency
and retiring, he had played roles in theatre
club productions and had been named Volunteer of the Year.

"Briefly," he said, "private citizens will
drive their own cars through the back roads
around mines—looking for wildfires and reporting them to a hotline by cell phone.
They will drive in three-hour patrols, around
an area divided into four segments. Some
of our civic leaders, upon hearing the plan,
volunteered immediately. Many more are

needed. Additional phone lines have been hooked up here at the station, and committee members are waiting to sign you up and answer your questions."

He mentioned Amanda Goodwinter, Derek Cuttlebrink, Dr. Diane Lanspeak, Whannell MacWhannell, Scott Gippel, and others. The roster of prominent names inspired action, and new names were broadcast as fast as they volunteered. Kemple answered questions:

"Yes, you can request daylight or nighttime hours. . . . You'll be given a detailed map of your segment. . . . If you don't have a cell phone, one will be provided. . . . About gas? Good question. Anyone driving two or more three-hour patrols can claim gas mileage from a kitty established by the K Fund. . . . Yes, by all means, take a partner—neighbor, friend, family member—to help with the firespotting. The first three-hour patrol is your donation to the cause. . . . Glad you mentioned that. MCCC students who volunteer will receive credits for community service. Cars will be identified by a small white pennant on the right front fender. Smile when you see one!"

Kemple made a final reminder: "Scheduling cars for twenty-four hours a day is tricky business and allows for no last-minute cancellations or no-shows. When you volunteer, you are protecting your county and your home. . . . Also, bear in mind that this is not a long-term commitment. Your help is needed only until snow flies."

Qwilleran turned off the radio and said proudly, "Only in a closely knit county like this could you facilitate a project so fast. Refresh your drink, Kirt?"

There was a shattering crash!

Nightingale jumped to his feet. "My God! What's that?"

Qwilleran glanced upward and saw Koko on the balcony railing, staring down at the mess he had created.

Kirt followed his glance. "Sorry! Gotta get out of here. Thanks for the drink." He rushed to the front door.

Qwilleran stroked his moustache. As a host he should feel embarrassed, and yet Nightingale's frantic exit was not enlisting his sympathy. Nevertheless, he would write a note of apology. It was partly his own fault; he had forgotten that Koko knew how to operate a lever-type door handle. And

Koko was only teasing, playing cat and mouse. The cat sensed a likely victim. Perhaps it was a mistake to let Fran Brodie put such objects on a balcony railing. The fact was: The row of five pots looked *good!* Now there were four.

Qwilleran phoned Polly and related the incident, then waited for her reaction.

She paused. "I know I should feel chagrined, but . . . why do I find it comic? I hope you had hidden the glove box."

"Have no fear. What do you think about the Citizens' Fire Watch?"

"*Better to light one small candle than to curse the darkness,* as the saying goes. Will you volunteer for a patrol?"

"Most likely I'll ride shotgun with Wetherby."

five

Two topics of conversation occupied downtown Pickax on Tuesday: the Citizens' Fire Watch and the loss of Eddington Smith. Townfolk were filled with sorrow on the one hand and hope on the other as they shared their thoughts at the post office, a civic meeting place. Built in Moose County's heyday, when Pickax expected to become a northern Chicago, its interior walls had been covered with murals in the 1930s—a federal project to give work to unemployed artists during the Great Depression. The post office and the bookstore were the city's two tourist attractions.

Qwilleran bought some postage stamps—and listened:

"The college president volunteered to take a fire patrol."

"Those two new doctors signed up."

"In our family we have three on patrol. I just pray: Dear Lord, don't let the wind rise!"

"The kids wanted to stay home from school so they could fire-watch with their daddy."

"Eddington was a nice little old man, but he didn't eat right, and I told him so."

"Can't be healthy—breathin' all that dust."

"Wonder what'll happen to his cat."

"Wonder what'll happen to his books."

Qwilleran, still astonished at the terms of Eddington's will, walked to Book Alley to view his inheritance. The bookstore glittered in the middle of the block like a crown jewel. On either side were nineteenth-century storefronts with tall windows. On one side were Albert's Dry Cleaning and Granny's Sweet Shop. She knew everyone's weakness; Mr. Q liked dark chocolate with nuts. On the other side were Gilda's Gift Shop and Brenda's

Unisex Hair Salon. Qwilleran patronized an old-fashioned barber with a revolving barber pole in front of his shop.

A sign in the bookstore window said CLOSED. It was dark inside, but the movement of a waving tail could be glimpsed in the gloom. Winston had been fed and was doing his dusting chores as usual.

Albert saw Qwilleran and opened the door. "Mr. Q! Your pants are ready!"

Qwilleran walked across the street. "Well, Albert, what are we going to do without Eddington?"

The dry cleaner shook his head. "That store was the lifeblood of this block. People came from all over to see it. Not too long ago a real estate guy from Bixby came around and wanted to buy it. Not a chance! Then he wanted to buy the storefronts, but our landlord wouldn't sell. No telling what they'd do—tear the whole block down, maybe, and build a strip mall."

"Winston seems to be all right."

"Yes, I see a girl coming to feed him."

"We should run a sob story about Winston with his photo, and find a new home for him," Qwilleran said.

"If you want to go in and see him," Albert said, "Edd always left the key under the doormat at the back door."

"May I use your phone?" Qwilleran called the photo lab at the *Something* and requested a shot of Eddington Smith's cat for the next day's deadline. "Not a mug shot," he stipulated. "He looks too ferocious. Preferably broadside, showing the plumed tail. The key is under the doormat at the rear, and be sure the cat doesn't run out."

Before leaving the block Qwilleran had a last look at the bookstore, wondering if— possibly—the college would accept the property and set up a work-and-learn project for students. Not a bad idea! Polly could give the benefit of her library science training, and Kirt could lecture on rare books. There was plenty of time to consider it. How long the estate would be in probate was anyone's guess.

The bookseller's funeral was a small one, as the modest old man would wish. Eddington Smith was laid to rest in a hilltop cemetery beyond the city limits— alongside his father. The elder Smith had been a door-to-door book salesman, bringing dictionaries and encyclopedias to countryfolk who had little schooling. Years later their purchases turned up in estate sales and then Eddington's shop, many of them as good as new.

The pastor of the Little Stone Church officiated at the funeral, and Qwilleran said a few words:

"Books were Eddington's life. Although he was not a reader himself, his mission was to supply books to readers and find readers for books. His building on Book Alley had been his grandfather's blacksmith shop, and it was a long leap from shoeing horses to binding books, but it was part of Edd's passion for books—to make an old book new again.

"As a person he was more of a friend than a businessman—always generous, steadfast, and kind. Whenever one of his customers passed on, he would say, 'There is a better land—far, far away.' And his seamy face would radiate a moment's joy as if he heard the song of angels. As we say farewell to Eddington, let us bid him godspeed to a better land—far, far away."

The few mourners walked quietly down the hill to their cars.

Qwilleran did Polly's grocery shopping, ensuring himself an invitation to dinner, and then went home to read his newspaper. On the editorial page he found a letter that surprised him:

To the Editor—Compliments to the Shafthouse Preservation Initiative on their success in having the abandoned mines declared historic places. We should all cheer Saturday's ceremony that dedicated the bronze plaques. Our mining heritage is unique. Let us not forget the miners' villages that surrounded the mines—the miners lining up at dawn to climb down a ladder into the lower depths—working like dogs for ten hours—climbing back up a thousand feet of ladder with blackened faces and empty stomachs—sometimes perishing in mine explosions that left whole villages fatherless. When we admire the cubistic architecture of the shafthouses, let us not forget the human sacrifice that allowed vast fortunes to be made for a few.

It was the signature that took him by surprise: Don Exbridge of Suffix Township. To dramatize the moment, another pot of geraniums fell from the balcony railing and crashed on the living room floor. He looked up to see a boldly impudent Koko enjoying his mischief.

There was no point in scolding; it had been folly to put the plants there in the first place. It was one of those "decorator touches" that Qwilleran succumbed to once in a while simply because Fran was glib, glamorous, and Brodie's daughter.

He swept up the debris and returned to his newspaper, only to discover the editorial page torn into shreds. What's more, Koko was right there, waiting to take credit for his depredations. The cat had oblique ways of communicating, and this could mean one of two things: Either he wanted shredded paper in his commode instead of the expensive dustproof litter that came in large bags . . . or he was saying that Don Exbridge's letter was a fake.

Qwilleran agreed with the latter. The sentimentality, the caring about heritage, even the word "cubistic" were all out of character for the bottom-liner who couldn't care less about history, environment, and the arts. Who was his ghostwriter? And what was it all about?

Qwilleran discussed the matter with Polly when he reported for dinner.

"I'll read a letter to the editor, and you guess who wrote it."

She guessed several members of the historical society and the genealogy club.

"Don Exbridge!" he announced.

"What's happened to him?" Polly gasped.

"Either he's been hit on the head, or he's going to be a father for the first time, or he's hired a spin doctor to give Donex & Associates a new corporate image. What's on the menu tonight?"

"Only leftovers," she said. "A ragout of last week's chicken soup and this weekend's cassoulet, with garlic croutons and a sprinkling of goat cheese. I hope you like it."

"Polly, you could open a restaurant with your leftovers! You could call it Leftovers Inc., or Deja Vu, or Not Again!"

They savored the ragout in silence for a few minutes, and then she said, "Those were beautiful words you spoke at Eddington's funeral."

"Glad to see your Dear Ladies attended." That was their private name for the white-haired, well-bred, conservative, wealthy women who served on the library board of directors.

"Yes, it was sweet of them. Who was the young woman with Mr. Barter?"

"Cynthia, the law clerk who's feeding Winston in the interim. She asked to attend. The man in a plaid shirt was Albert, the dry cleaner."

"I thought I recognized him. I was in Book Alley this noon, having my hair done during my lunch hour, and Brenda told me some wild news: Don Exbridge's wife has filed for divorce!"

"His second or third?"

"He's had only two. She's the mousy one we met last year when they invited us to dinner. She reminded me of my mother-in-law, who squeezed toothpaste onto her husband's toothbrush every day for forty years. Such wifely devotion!"

"Correction! The elder Mrs. Duncan was a thrifty Scot who didn't like to see dentifrice wasted."

"Oh Qwill! You're so cynical!"

"Not at all. A survey shows that men use toothpaste more lavishly than women do, and budget-conscious wives are on a cost-cutting campaign that alarms marketing specialists and interests psychologists. A fifty percent cut in toothpaste consumption could be a blow to the economy."

"You're inventing this, Qwill!" Polly laughed. "You're plotting another hoax on your readers. You'll have them measuring the toothpaste on family toothbrushes and sending their reports to the *Something* on postal cards."

"You have no faith in me," he said as he helped himself to seconds. "What's that on the sideboard? It looks like Maggie's French martini pitcher."

"It's yours now. She brought it to the library today. She wants very much for you to have it."

He gasped. "She shouldn't have! It's too much! But I accept."

Qwilleran declined dessert—stewed figs with yogurt—saying he had to take a nap before fire-watching with Wetherby. He left shortly, swinging the pitcher by its sturdy handle. "Wait till Koko and Yum Yum see it!

They'll know it came from a household with five cats."

As it turned out, the Siamese knew not only the provenance of the pitcher, but also the sex of Maggie's cats—all females. Koko nuzzled it enthusiastically, but Yum Yum backed away and bushed her tail.

At eleven P.M. Qwilleran gave the cats their bedtime snack, then led the ceremonial march upstairs, with Koko second in line and Yum Yum trailing a lazy third. He ushered them into their room, said goodnight, turned out the light and closed the door. This was the "tucking-in" ritual.

In his boyhood his mother had tucked him in nightly—listening to his prayers, tucking the bedcovers under his chin, giving his forehead a goodnight kiss, wishing him pleasant dreams. He wondered how much of it was motherly affection and how much was a motherly prayer-check. He hated to hurt the feelings of the only parent he had, but on his tenth birthday he ventured that he was too old for tucking-in. She understood.

The Siamese had no such objections, and after they were tucked in, Qwilleran dressed for fire-watching and awaited the signal from his neighbor.

"All set to go, Joe. Would a thermos of hot coffee be appropriate?"

"Brilliant idea!"

They rode in Wetherby's van, which had a white flag flying from a front fender, affixed by a magnet. "We'll be cruising at a slower speed than other vehicle traffic."

"Actually, there won't be much traffic at this hour—on the secondary roads we'll be traveling. The flags were borrowed from Dingleberry Funeral Home. City funerals don't use flags anymore. The procession races to the cemetery at normal speed, with a police escort. Somehow, that doesn't seem respectful, but I'm just a country boy from Horseradish."

Following their map, they zigzagged through back roads and phoned "all clear" to the courthouse operator at each checkpoint. Traffic was light except for a half hour when the bars closed. Once, Wetherby stopped and shone his headlights on a new building that looked like a Swiss chalet. "The new curling club," he said. "I don't curl, but I'm a member, and that's where I go to relax. We should go some night."

"What facilities do they have?" Qwilleran asked.

"Three rinks, spectator gallery, warming room with bar, locker room . . ."

"I've seen pictures of players on the ice with large stones and little brooms. What's it all about? In twenty-five words or less."

"Are you counting?" Wetherby asked. "Well, the idea is to slide the stone across the ice and into the target area. A skilled player can make the stone do tricks—curl around another stone, take out an opponent's stone. Fascinating!"

"What does a stone weigh?"

"Forty-two pounds, carved from Scottish granite."

"Do players have their own stones and take them home like bowling balls?"

"No. Stones have to be refrigerated or they'll melt the ice."

Apart from the conversation, it had been a dull expedition. In the first twenty-four hours of the Fire Watch there had been only one brushfire, resulting when a truck accident knocked down a power line. There had been no smoldering or black smoke in any of the four Mine Zones. The volunteer fire departments had it easy.

But the night was not over.

After saying goodnight to his neighbor, Qwilleran unlocked his front door and saw a scene of destruction. A table lamp had been toppled and was hanging upside-down from its cord. The Danish rug was bunched. Red pillows, wooden apples, magazines, and desktop papers were on the floor. Geraniums were in the kitchen sink.

It meant only one thing, Qwilleran knew: a cat fit! . . . a prediction of trouble . . . probably the Big One. Having given the warning, Koko was lying on the mantel, exhausted. Yum Yum was hiding. Methodically Qwilleran began putting the room together again.

Halfway through his task he suddenly stopped and listened: a boom like a cannon shot . . . a rumble like thunder! He rushed outdoors. In minutes the fire trucks could be heard—racing from various directions, converging on Pickax. A sickening thought occurred to him: It was the Mackintosh Inn—again! A year before—when it was the Pickax Hotel—it had been bombed by a psychopath from Down Below. Already a red glow was building in the black sky.

He snatched a jacket and his keys and ran for his van.

six

Downtown was ablaze with flashing lights and searchlights, and a three-block area was closed to traffic. A thick column of smoke was rising where flames had been contained. Qwilleran parked and walked closer. It was not the inn; was it the post office? His press card admitted him as far as the yellow tape, where he asked an officer, "Is it the post office?"

"No, Mr. Q. Behind the post office."

Incredible! Qwilleran thought. He skirted the yellow tape to the north end of Book Alley. The bookstore was a roofless shell, belching smoke. Firefighters were pouring water on the roofs of nearby buildings.

Flickers of light on the pavement came from shattered glass.

"What happened?" Qwilleran asked a firefighter with a soot-covered face who was taking a breather.

"Explosion, Mr. Q. Roof blew off. Books went up like a bonfire. Nothing left but the stone walls."

It was the voice of a sheep farmer he knew. "You're—you're—"

"Terence Ogilvie. Black Creek Volunteer Fire Department."

"Yes, of course." Qwilleran was remembering his visit to the back room where Eddington lived and did his bookbinding. A kerosene stove for heat. A propane burner for cooking. A big box of matches. And Winston! "There was a cat!" he said in alarm.

"Couldn't possibly survive."

Two fire trucks from outlying villages were pulling away. "How long will you stay here, Terence?"

"Some of us will stay all night, watching for hot spots." They were standing with their backs to a vacant lot overgrown with weeds. "There's a candidate for a fire right there! First thing we did, we hosed it down. All it would take is one spark!"

Something made Qwilleran turn abruptly to look at the lot. "Winston!" he shouted.

A large, black, bedraggled animal was prowling toward him through the wet weeds.

"That's Winston! You'd never recognize him!"

Hearing his name, knowing the voice, associating it with a frequent can of sardines, Winston approached Qwilleran confidently.

"He's a mess! And if he was blown through the roof, he could be hurt. If I could get hold of him, I'd take him to the pet hospital."

"Cats are resilient. The question is: How did he get out? Where's your car, Mr. Q?"

"On Main Street, two blocks away."

"Bring it around. I'll keep an eye on him."

Shepherds empathize with animals, Qwilleran had learned, and animals trust them. In ten minutes he was backing the van up to the yellow tape, opening the tailgate, and taking out an old blanket.

"Careful, Mr. Q! You could get scratched! And he's covered with soot."

"Good cat! Good cat!" Qwilleran mumbled as he gathered Winston in the blanket. A switching tail slapped him in the face and across his newly cleaned suede jacket.

As he drove away, his hands were black; the steering wheel was black; and he left a black smudge on the emergency bell at the pet hospital.

The night attendant who came to the door exclaimed, "Mr. Q! What happened to your face?"

"I have a cat in my car who survived a fire and explosion."

"How big?"

"Big!"

Using a large plastic carrier, she transported Winston to the emergency room.

"He doesn't look seriously injured," she reported. "I'll clean him up, and the doctor will examine him first thing in the morning. What's his name?"

"Winston Churchill."

Early the next morning Qwilleran phoned the attorney at home. "Sorry to wake you, Bart. Have you heard about Book Alley?"

"What? . . . What?" was the sleepy response.

"Explosion in the bookstore. Whole building gutted. All the books destroyed."

"When? . . . When?"

"Three o'clock this morning. I heard the *boom* and hurried downtown. Winston is safe. He's at the pet hospital. You might notify Cynthia she doesn't have to feed him."

"Yes . . . Yes."

"Shall I take the initiative in finding him a new home?"

"Please . . . Please."

Barter was not at his best when rudely awakened.

"I'll get back to you if problems arise," Qwilleran said, and then returned to his own concerns and responsibilities. The explosion and fire would be front-page news in that day's paper, and it would be well to write a sidebar on Winston. He reflected that, ironically, the disaster solved the problem of what to do with the bookstore. He wondered, skeptically, about the Bixby real estate agent who wanted to buy the premises. He pondered, in amazement,

Koko's cat fit preceding the explosion by a few minutes.

At nine o'clock he reached the veterinarian.

"Miraculously," she said, "he has no injuries, not even singed fur. Are you sure he was in the building?"

"Winston never went out. He doesn't know what 'out' means."

"And his vital signs are normal. You can pick him up any time."

Qwilleran cleared his throat while doing some quick thinking. He said, "I'd like to board him with you for twenty-four hours, doctor, for observation, and while we arrange for adoption."

"You won't have any trouble finding a home for him, after the story gets out."

"Very true," he replied ruefully. How well he knew, as a journalist, how people scramble to adopt an animal with celebrity status: the kitten trapped in a sewer pipe for three days, or the stray dog that saved a family of five. Any family would want Winston, but would he want them?

He called Maggie Sprenkle for help. "Have you heard a newscast this morning?"

"Isn't it dreadful? And the poor man hardly in his grave!"

"You'll be glad to know his cat escaped and is okay. I'm boarding him at the hospital until we figure out what to do about adoption. He'll be on the front page today, and he'll get hundreds of offers."

"I never thought of that," she said.

"He can't possibly have been blasted through the roof, but if someone gets the idea that he was airborne, it'll be on TV, and then we can expect calls from all over the country. We should find him a home before he goes public."

"Yes! I'll make a few phone calls—"

"Bear in mind, Maggie, that he'll be happiest in a quiet home with elderly people, no other pets, and a large library."

Qwilleran's next call went to Junior Goodwinter at the *Something*.

"Hey!" said the managing editor. "Our night man said he saw you at the fire last night! What were you doing there at three A.M.?"

"Rescuing the cat, and that's why I'm calling. Everyone will want to adopt him. There'll be a rumor that he was blasted through the roof, and that will add to his glamour. But it's not true. He escaped unharmed. I don't know how, but he did."

"What do you want me to do?"

"Don't go for the big story. Tell the truth. The resident cat was rescued unharmed and has been adopted."

"Is that a fact?" the editor asked.

"It will be, by the time you go to press."

The phone rang and rang. Good friends and casual acquaintances, aware of Qwilleran's fondness for the bookstore, called to commiserate. The Siamese knew he was preoccupied and left him alone. Finally he stopped answering the intrusive signal, and the message-taker worked overtime. The only call he returned was the one from Maggie Sprenkle:

"Good news!" she said. "The Bethunes on Pleasant Street will be happy to have Winston. They'll pick him up at the hospital and pay his bill. He's a retired chemist. They were regular customers of Eddington's. And they go to my church."

"I could ask no better recommendation, Maggie. Thank you for expediting it. And how can I thank you enough for the pitcher? It occupies a place of honor in my living room."

"My pleasure, I assure you."

It had been a sleepless and emotional ordeal for Qwilleran: Koko's catfit . . . the explosion . . . the thought of thousands of books reduced to black ash . . . his fear for Winston, followed by the cat's rescue and adoption. A nap would have been in order, but Qwilleran had a tiger by the tail. He could not let go. He drove back to Pickax for a painful look at Book Alley in daylight.

Boarding was being erected around Eddington's property, including the small backyard. The street had been cleaned of shattered glass, since mail trucks used it for access to the back door of the post office. The storefronts now had plywood where their windows had been, and the shopkeepers were moving out. The *Something* was not yet on the street, but hourly newscasts on WPKX ended with the usual words: Police are investigating.

It was Qwilleran's cue to go to see his friend, the police chief, and tell what he knew. Andrew Brodie was a big Scot who looked more comfortable in a kilt than a cop's uniform. He beckoned Qwilleran into his office.

"How come you didn't play the bagpipe at Eddington's funeral, Andy?"

"Nobody asked me to. Know anything about the fire?"

"This may be hearsay, Andy, but I was told that a guy from Bixby was trying to buy the whole block for redevelopment. Nobody would sell. Then Edd died, and the bookstore—the kingpin of the block—blew up! It doesn't take much imagination to suspect arson."

Brodie grunted.

"And that's not all. Eddington's cat escaped unharmed. How—and why—did he get out? He was an indoor cat. Did he sense danger when an unauthorized stranger unlocked the door and came in? Did he sneak out and hide in the weeds? The key was under the doormat. That's where everyone puts the key, isn't it? In Moose County, at least. No matter how much you try to educate them, people will still leave their door keys under the doormat and the car keys in the ignition. So I say the arsonist is a local and not a pyromaniac from Down Below."

"Good!" said Brodie. "That narrows the suspects down to a few thousand."

Qwilleran started to leave the office. "Don't say I never gave you a tip!"

Loafing around Main Street, the coffee shops, and the post office, Qwilleran heard the man on the street:

"Downtown won't be the same without that building!"

"I remember it ever since I was a li'l tyke!"

"People came from all over and took pictures of it."

"My old man said it used to be a blacksmith shop."

There was not one word about the thousands of books that had been reduced to ash.

Qwilleran managed to take a nap before dressing for dinner with the Morghans. Barry, manager of the Mackintosh Inn, was renting the apartment in the Klingenschoen carriage house. He had the careful grooming and cordial manner of his profession. His brother, Theo, the dermatologist, was a young man with a neatly clipped beard that brought to Qwilleran's mind Polly's theory: patients have more confidence in a doctor with a neatly clipped beard. The doctor's wife, Misty, was all smiles and curly brown hair and mischievous brown eyes. Like Qwilleran himself, they were Chicagoans, with a city veneer that was recognizable in a small town. Qwilleran's veneer was wearing thin.

The conversation started with the usual get-acquainted formula: "Yes, we've bought a big old house on Pleasant Street. . . . No. We haven't any kids yet, but we want a family, and this looks like a good community for rearing them. . . . Yes, we have pets. Two Yorkies. . . . No, we've never lived in a town smaller than Chicago."

"I think it'll be fun!" said Misty.

"But we have a lot to learn," Theo added.

"For one thing," Qwilleran said, "you can expect your patients to call you Dr. Theo—not Dr. Morghan. It combines neighborliness with respect."

"Everyone seems very friendly," Misty commented.

"True. And everyone will want to know

everything about you. Data will then be exchanged in the coffee shops, on the church steps, at the post office, and over the phone. It's not gossip. It's caring and sharing. . . . Got it?"

"Got it!" the couple said in unison.

"By the same token, never speak unkindly about anyone, because you may be talking to a brother-in-law, second cousin, neighbor, or golf partner."

Barry said, "Qwill, when I first came here, you told me to keep my ears open and my mouth shut. Priceless advice! In the same class with: Look both ways before crossing the street."

The host served cocktails, and Qwilleran had to explain Squunk water—from a local mineral spring with a believe-it-or-not history.

"Tell it!" Misty urged.

"You'll have to wait and buy the book. It's one of my collection of Moose County legends to be titled *Short & Tall Tales*."

Then Theo asked about the mayoral election campaign. He had seen some unusual posters and newspaper ads.

"Juicy question!" Qwilleran said with relish. "In a nutshell, the incumbent was a

high school principal who resigned following a scandal involving girl students—
resigned without censure, because *his
mother was a Goodwinter!* Four Goodwinter brothers founded Pickax and operated the most famous, or infamous, mine.
Ancestors count heavily here.''

''I can see that!''

''So Mrs. Goodwinter's little boy grew up
to be mayor, elected and re-elected because . . . all together now!''

''His mother was a Goodwinter!'' the
other three chimed.

''He earns his living as an investment
counselor.''

''A handsome dog,'' Barry said. ''Every
time he comes into the inn, people fawn
over him.''

''Although they whisper about his integrity when they're in safe company.''

''This is great!'' said Barry with a roguish
grin.

''Now we come to the good part,'' Qwilleran went on. ''For a long time we've had
a spunky, outspoken woman on the city
council. She could challenge the mayor
with impunity because her *father* was a

Goodwinter. That gave her an edge by local standards."

Misty asked, "Is she the Amanda Goodwinter who has the design studio? I've only met her assistant, but they're handling my artwork."

"She's the one! Her friends have finally convinced her to run for the mayor's office. It's a joke! He's good-looking, suave, and well dressed; Amanda looks grouchy and dresses like a scarecrow. That's the kind of individuality the locals enjoy. Do you have today's paper, Barry?"

Qwilleran showed them two campaign ads: a photo of a handsome man with the slogan *Re-elect Mayor Blythe!,* and a caricature of a witch with the slogan *We'd Rather Have Amanda!*

Misty clapped her hands, and Theo said, "I hope it's not too late to register to vote."

The doorbell rang. Chef Wingo was sending over a paella—a dish of chicken, rice, shrimp, and the Spanish sausage called chorizo. During dinner, conversation touched on many topics.

Barry said that the country club was giving a reception for the two doctors and their wives. Theo's partner was an avid golfer.

Theo said that he and Misty preferred curling as a sport. "I discovered it while in med school in Michigan. We want to join the curling club."

Misty remarked about the spectacular murals in the Pickax post office, and Qwilleran explained, "They were painted during the Great Depression, as part of the federal works project, depicting Moose County's history: mining, lumbering, quarrying, shipbuilding, and farming."

Barry was amazed at the huge number of volunteers signing up for the Citizens' Fire Watch. An editorial in the *Something* had said, "The blood of pioneers still flows in the veins of their descendants, giving them a sense of community responsibility."

Misty said that the art center had invited her to give a demonstration lecture on batik painting.

"I have one of your wall hangings," Qwilleran told her. "Fran Brodie sent it over to give the living room a splash of color."

"Are they robins? I did two hangings on that theme, titled 'Two Robins with Worm' and 'Two Robins without Worm.' Which do you have?"

"With," he said.

"That's my favorite. It's more dynamic."

After one of Chef Wingo's simple desserts—melon cubes with lime sorbet and mango sauce—the party broke up in a flurry of handshakes and pleasant words, and Qwilleran hurried home for a dish of ice cream with chocolate sauce and redskin peanuts.

As he unlocked the front door he could hear the urgent baritone yowling in the foyer. Koko was telling him that there was a message on the answering machine.

It was from Rhoda Tibbitt. "Homer and I were shocked to hear about the bookstore, Qwill. Eddington had told us he was leaving it to you. Do you have time to drop in for tea tomorrow afternoon? We have some information that Homer thinks you ought to know."

It was too late to return the call. The Tibbitts retired at eight o'clock.

There was another message, too. Polly's voice said, "Are you free tomorrow evening? Maggie wants us to have dinner with her. Dr. Zoller will be there. She apologizes for the short notice. Her housekeeper, by the way, is an excellent cook." Qwilleran was available. He had always wanted to meet Dr. Zoller . . . and he was always interested in a free dinner.

seven

How did Winston escape from the doomed building? Unanswered questions always irked Qwilleran, and he spent a restless night. At nine A.M., when Roger MacGillivray would be reporting for work, he phoned the photo lab at the *Something*.

"Roger, compliments on your morning-after photo in yesterday's paper. It was not only graphic but heartbreaking!"

"Gee, thanks, Qwill. How'd you like Winston's portrait? Ironically I got that shot the day before the explosion, for the new adopt-a-pet feature."

"That's one reason I'm calling. When you

went to the back door, did Winston make any attempt to get out of the store?"

"If he had, I would've run a mile. You know how I am about cats. No, in fact he didn't make an appearance for a while. It turned out he was in his sandbox."

"Well, your broadside shot of him was perfect—from his bold whiskers to his flamboyant tail."

"Yeah, I was glad to see they ran it three columns."

Qwilleran said, "He's already been adopted by a couple living on Pleasant Street."

"Who?"

"The Bethunes."

"Sure. I know their son. Swell people . . . Thanks for calling. I've gotta run. There's a nine-thirty on the board."

Qwilleran's next call went to the law office, where he talked to Cynthia. "Have you heard that Winston has a new home?"

"I'm so glad," she said. "He's a gorgeous cat! If I had a place of my own, I would've adopted him in a minute."

"I take it that you two got along."

"I only knew he was glad to see me at

mealtime," she said. "Who's taking him, Mr. Q?"

"The Bethunes on Pleasant Street."

"Really? She's my boyfriend's aunt! Very nice woman. Hope she doesn't spoil him."

"One question, Cynthia. When you went to feed him, did he ever try to run out the back door?"

"Never! I always opened the door cautiously, though—just in case—but he was a very cool cat."

Qwilleran went downtown for breakfast at Rennie's and eavesdropped on conversations:

"Too bad! It was our biggest tourist attraction. . . . It was feldspar, you know. It shatters like eggshells. . . . It's a blessing the old man wasn't here to see it . . . They should do something about those kerosene heaters!"

Only at the library, where he went next, were they mourning the loss of the books. Clerks and volunteers were always glad to see him—the "Qwill Pen" columnist, Klingenschoen heir, boss's boyfriend. "She's not here," they said. "She had a dental appointment."

They lavished attention on him: Showed him Mr. Smith's last bookbinding project for the library. Demonstrated the new gadget for checking out books. Inquired about Koko and Yum Yum. Pointed out the new exhibit of antique inkwells. Asked who was his favorite author. Brought the feline mascots, Mac and Katie, to say hello.

He responded with amiable nods and quips and murmurs of approval. He said his housemates had stopped shedding—in preparation for the Big One. To two gray-haired volunteers who were fussing over old photographs for an exhibit, he said lightly, "Need any help, ladies?"

"Yes!" they replied in unison and proceeded to talk at once. "The men in this photo . . . there's no identification . . . except for the one in front. He's Governor Witherspoon. . . . It was taken in 1928."

"I'm afraid I wasn't around then," Qwilleran said with good humor.

Without blinking they went on. "People like to know who's in these old photos. It may be an ancestor. . . . Their great-grandpa may have been a friend of the governor. . . . They can bring the kids to the library to see a picture of their great-great-grandpa, photographed with the governor."

"I see." Qwilleran began to realize the seriousness of the matter. "I'll bet Homer Tibbitt would recognize them." One man was carrying a ledger; two were in sheriff's uniforms; another had a hunting dog.

"Mr. Tibbitt used to come to the library every day, doing research, you know. Now that he's moved to Ittibittiwassee Estates, we never see him—do we, Dora? . . . No. I thought he'd passed away. He's almost a hundred."

Qwilleran said, "I'm going out that way this afternoon. Do you want me to take the photo along?"

"That would be wonderful! We'll put it in an envelope."

Homer, the nonagenarian historian, and Rhoda, ten years his junior, had married late. Both had been educators. Neither had been married before. For visitors they always staged a comic act of marital banter. Everyone knew they were a devoted couple.

The retirement village where they now

lived was out in the country—a four-story
building with steeply pitched roof, looking
somewhat like a Swiss resort hotel. When
Qwilleran arrived with Gov. Witherspoon's
photo and a bunch of flowers for Rhoda, he
parked in the visitors' lot and was approaching the building when he saw Mayor
Gregory Blythe coming out.

"Good afternoon, Mayor," he said.
"Have you been rallying your constitu-
ents?"

"It doesn't hurt to keep the home fires
burning," said the impeccably groomed
candidate.

Blythe, during his three terms, had pro-
moted the annexation of surrounding town-
ships for various reasons, one of which
was to add voting districts.

"Met hizzoner in the parking lot," Qwilleran said when Rhoda admitted him to
their apartment. "Was he scrounging votes
or selling stocks and bonds?"

"I tell you one thing: He won't get a
nickel of my money," Homer railed in his
high-pitched voice. "He comes here to
charm the widows out of their pensions
and their husbands' life insurance."

"Don't get excited, Homer," his wife

said. "We'll all have a nice cup of chamomile tea."

"She's trying to poison me with that stuff!" he said.

"That being the case," Qwilleran said, "don't drink it until you answer a question for the Pickax library. They miss your daily visits." He explained the situation and showed the photo of Gov. Witherspoon and friends.

"That's the Guv, all right. No mistaking those big ears! I know all these others, too. Can't think of their names. Rhoda's good at names; I recognize faces. Rhoda!"

She came hurrying from the kitchen. "Yes, that's Gov. Witherspoon. My friends and I thought he was terribly romantic-looking. The two men on the second step I know very well. They're the Brown brothers—"

"Which Brown brothers?" Qwilleran interrupted.

"There was only one Brown family," she explained sweetly. "The one with the rifle and the dog is . . . It's on the tip of my tongue: Fred Bryce—or Brook—or Broom—"

"Or Brown," Qwilleran suggested.

"The funny thing is—I know the name of his dog! Diana! Goddess of the Hunt!"

"Makes sense."

Homer had lost interest and was dozing off.

In a loud voice Qwilleran said, "But all this is ancient history. Let us talk about Eddington Smith."

"Dear Eddington! A gentle soul!" Rhoda said softly.

"He wasn't a reader, but he knew and loved books," her husband added in a voice less strident than usual. "In his heyday he traveled all over the map. Certain estate liquidators used to save cartons of the best books for him. But he was getting old and tired, and so was his truck."

"He'd come and have dinner with us and talk about his family," she said.

"Worshiped his father, a door-to-door book salesman."

"His mother died early, and he was raised by his grandmother. Her husband was a blacksmith, and he built the feldspar building for them to live in. The smithy was in the backyard."

"Under a spreading chestnut tree?" Qwilleran asked.

"It happened to be a mighty oak," Homer said. "It was cut down when Edd asphalted the yard as a parking lot. He rented a few spaces for parking."

"You mentioned on the phone that you had some information—"

"Something his grandmother told him on her deathbed," Rhoda said. "We thought it might be a story for your collection of Moose County legends."

"I won't know till I hear it. Do you remember the details?"

"Between the two of us, I think we can remember how it went, but you'll have to write it in your own narrative style, Qwill."

He turned on his tape recorder.

On the way back to town he began dry-writing the story in his head. First he dropped off the photo of Gov. Witherspoon at the library.

"Sorry to be unsuccessful," he apologized to the volunteers. "But here's what I suggest: Feature it as a mystery photo. Invite the townfolk to bring their family albums to the library and see if they can match up any of the faces. I'll mention it in my column."

His idea was received with delight. Polly was back from the dentist, but he had no time to go up to her office. He wanted to go home and write *Secrets of the Blacksmith's Wife,* as told to Eddington Smith by his grandmother.

When Pickax was named the county seat—because of its central location—it was only a hamlet, but a building boom started almost overnight. The blacksmith, who made nails as well as horseshoes, could hardly keep up with the demand as ambitious settlers built dwellings and shops. Then one day he was kicked in the head by a horse and died on the spot. There was panic in Pickax! No blacksmith! No nails!

The next day, by a strange coincidence, a stranger walked into town—a big brawny man carrying a stick over his shoulder with a bundle tied on the end. He wore his hair longer than was the custom in Moose County, and at first he was viewed with suspicion. When he said he was a blacksmith, however, the townfolk changed their attitude.

Could he make nails?

Yes, he could make nails.

What was his name?

John.

John what?

He said, "Just John. That's all the name you need to make nails."

This was somewhat irregular, but they needed nails, so the local officials put their heads together and listed him on the town rolls as John B. Smith, the middle initial standing for "Black."

When Longfellow wrote "The smith a mighty man is he," he might have been writing about John B. He was tall and broad-shouldered, with *large and sinewy hands,* and his muscles were *strong as iron bands*. No one dared criticize his long hair. Furthermore, he was twenty-two and good-looking, and all the young women in town were after him. It was not long before he married Emma, who could read and write. They had six children, although only three reached adulthood—not an unusual situation in those days. He built them a house of quarry stone with a front of feldspar that sparkled like diamonds on a sunny day. It was much admired by the other settlers, who liked novelty.

The smithy was in the backyard, and there John worked industriously, turning out tools, wagon wheels, cookpots, horseshoes, and nails. He was a good provider and went to chapel with his family twice a week. Emma was the envy of most women in town.

Once in a while he told her he had to visit his old mother in Lockmaster, and he would get on his horse and ride south, staying a week or more. The local gossips said he had another wife down there, but Emma trusted him, and he always brought her a pretty shawl or a nice piece of cloth to make into a dress.

Then came a time when he failed to return. There was no way of tracing his whereabouts, but Emma was sure he had been killed by highwaymen who wanted to steal his horse and gold watch. Lockmaster—with its fur-trading and gold-mining—offered rich pickings for robbers. Someone from the next town wanted to buy John's anvil and tools, but Emma refused to sell.

Yet, as time went on and she thought about his past behavior, she remembered how he used to go out into the yard in the middle of the night without a lantern. She never asked questions, and he never explained, but she could hear the sound of digging. That was not so unusual; there were no banks, and valuables were often buried. Then she recalled that it always happened after a visit to his old mother.

Emma was fired by curiosity, and she went out to the smithy with a shovel. It was dark, but she went without a lantern rather than arouse further gossip. Most of the yard was trampled hard as a rock. There was one spot near the big tree where she tried digging. There were tree roots. She found another spot.

Then, just as she was about to give up, her shovel struck metal. She dropped to her knees and began scraping the soil furiously with her bare hands, gradually exposing an iron chest. With her hands trembling and heart pounding, she opened the lid. The chest was filled with gold coins! Frightened by the sight, she closed the lid and knelt there, hugging her arms in thought—deep   thought. . . . There had been a dark rag on top of the gold. Once more she opened the lid— just a few inches—and reached in stealthily as if afraid to touch the coins. Pulling out the rag, she took it indoors to examine by lamplight.

It was bright red. It was the red bandanna that a pirate tied around his head.

She went back to the yard, covered the chest with soil, stamping it down with her feet. The next day she had the yard paved with cobblestones.

Emma had always wondered where her husband had acquired his gold watch.

And Qwilleran wondered, as he wrote the last sentence, how freely had Eddington chatted with the strangers who spent hours on his ladders? Had he told them his grandmother's tale?

* * *

The Siamese seemed to be spending many of their waking hours on the coffee table, mesmerized by the French martini pitcher. While Yum Yum hung back warily, Koko gave it a nearsighted, nose-twitching examination. No doubt he thought he saw movement inside. The thick glass, its voluptuous shape, the ever-changing quality and direction of the light source, and his own shifting position—all produced an effect of activity inside the innocent jug.

Koko was hanging over it as if it were a crystal ball, and Qwilleran wondered whimsically if the cat could read the future. He had to guard against taking the cat's prescience too seriously, so he said heartily, "Any excitement today? Did any river rats come up for a drink of water? I hope you didn't invite them in."

Koko and Yum Yum acted totally deaf. As always, on acquiring another legend for his collection, Qwilleran was exhilarated—until he thought, How can I publish this? It'll bring a horde of opportunists with jackhammers!

Membership in the Honorable Society of

Treasure Hunters had been growing since a few had struck it rich. Oldtimers in Moose County would rather bury their money in a coffee can in the backyard than entrust it to a bank. The sites of former outhouses were said to be particular treasure troves. The diggers went out after dark. It was a wholesome hobby, they said, affording fresh air, exercise, excitement, and sometimes rewards. Their enthusiasm was not shared, however, by property owners whose lawns, pastures, and fields of soybeans had been excavated.

Then Qwilleran thought, The Bixby realty agent (if that's what he was) may have had something in mind other than a strip mall. "Yow!" came a loud clear comment from Koko—either to corroborate Qwilleran's theory or remind him that dinner was overdue.

Qwilleran fed the Siamese and then dressed for Maggie's dinner party.

eight

Qwilleran picked up Polly for the drive to Maggie Sprenkle's dinner party, and as soon as they turned onto the highway, he asked, "What's new in your exciting young life?"

"I custom-ordered a sweater from Barb Ogilvie—for my sister, for Christmas. Camel tan with sculptured texture in the knit. Did you know that Barb is dating Barry Morghan? They met through Barry's sister-in-law, who's an artist."

"They sound like a likely pair," he said.

"Barb said she saw you going into the antique shop one day."

"Is that good or bad?"

"That all depends. Have you started collecting antiques? Or did you go to visit Susan Darling?" There had been a personality clash between the two women ever since Susan's brief term on the library board. Susan said the head librarian had unsophisticated taste; Polly said the antique dealer had never read a book in her life. It was the kind of feud that gave Qwilleran devilish amusement. He had to bite his tongue to resist telling Polly she had Susan's porcelain parrots.

He said, "I went in to congratulate her on being accepted for the New York show—but really to scrounge a cup of coffee. I saw a sampler I liked, and she gave it to me."

"What kind of sampler?" Polly asked sharply.

"You'll see, next time you come over. I also have a wall hanging over the fireplace, selected by Fran."

"What kind of hanging?"

"Wait and see." He was being mischievously perverse. Then to change the subject: "What's this dinner party all about?"

"Wait and see," Polly said smugly.

Maggie lived downtown in the Sprenkle

Building on Main Street. She and her late husband had lived on a large estate famous for its rose gardens, but she had sold the house, preferring to live in an apartment with rose-patterned carpet. The ground floor of the nineteenth-century building was rented to insurance and realty firms; the two upper floors had been transformed into a Victorian palace. Qwilleran had been there once before to meet her five cats named after well-known women: Sarah, Charlotte, Carrie, Flora, and Louisa May.

As he and Polly drove up to the building, he asked, "Shall we risk our lives and take the front stairs?" They were steep and narrow in the old style, with shallow treads made shallower by thick carpeting, rose-patterned to confuse the eye.

"Let's use the rear entrance and ride the elevator," she said. "I'm not yet ready to break my neck."

The elevator glided slowly and silently to the second floor and debouched the two passengers in a lavish foyer. Polly whispered, "Decorated by Amanda Goodwinter," and he muttered, "That figures."

The foyer was two stories high, with a carved staircase leading to the upper floor and an enormous chandelier hanging in the stairwell. It was a shower of crystal and amethyst pendants, said to have mystic powers of restoring one's energy.

The hostess, greeting them in a black velvet dress and the famous Sprenkle torsade of diamonds and pearls, said, "I stand under the chandelier every morning for a few minutes to recharge my batteries." It was a fact that she had an abundance of vitality and enthusiasm for her age.

At her urging Qwilleran tried it and announced facetiously that he could feel his hair standing on end and his moustache burgeoning. Polly declined, saying she had tried it before and was unable to sleep for three nights.

In the rose-patterned parlor introductions were made. The fourth member of the party was Henry Zoller, financial officer of XYZ Enterprises until his recent retirement. He had been a dentist and was still called Dr. Zoller in Moose County—but not to his face. Now he was sixtyish, distinguished-looking, well tanned, and conservative in clothing, manner, and speech.

"Please call me Henry," he said. "Maggie tells me I may call you Polly and Qwill. I admire you both for your professionalism. And Qwill! What you said about the IRS in your recent column on acronyms gave me a hearty chuckle. Have you had much response?"

"Only to have my last tax returned audited." It was not true, but it was a quip Qwilleran could not resist.

"To your health!" Zoller proposed when apéritifs were served.

They sat on red velvet–tufted chairs, set their drinks on the marble tops of carved tables, and looked at red walls hung with a fortune in oil paintings bought in Paris by an ancestral Sprenkle.

"Where are the ladies?" Polly asked, inquiring about the five well-fed cats that usually sat on the five parlor windowsills. Qwilleran had noticed there were no cat hairs on Maggie's black velvet, although she was a compulsive cat-hugger.

"They've retired to their boudoir upstairs," she said. Deftly she steered the conversation away from the Big One, Book Alley, the Citizens' Fire Watch, and even the Shafthouse Initiative. Instead they talked about golf, travel, art collecting, photography, dog racing in Florida, and the best restaurants in Chicago.

The housekeeper cooked and served: lobster bisque, filet of beef with sauced broccoli, a tossed green salad, and a white chocolate mousse.

After coffee, Qwilleran and Polly waited forty-five minutes before saying goodnight.

On the way home she said, "A half hour's grace is too short to be polite; an hour is too long to be comfortable."

Qwilleran agreed that the evening had seemed rather lengthy. "But the food was good. What did she do to the broccoli?"

"A light cheese sauce with bacon bits."

"Broccoli needs all the help it can get."

"Maggie and Henry have known each other a long time. When their spouses were living, the two couples went on cruises all over the world."

"What will he do now that he's retired? Go back to fixing teeth?"

"Probably play golf and bet on the dogs."

"Maggie seemed a little subdued tonight," Qwilleran said. "She hasn't been spending enough time under the chandelier."

* * *

As they drove through the Indian Village gates, Polly said, "Would you like to come in for a while?"

"How'd you like to come and see the sampler I swindled from Susan?" Qwilleran asked.

She agreed readily. She had been consumed by curiosity. As soon as he unlocked the door she went directly to the kitchen and stared—or glared—at the framed piece of stained linen laboriously embroidered by a young girl a hundred years ago.

By the constrained expression on her face he could read her mind.

"Don't you like it?" he teased. "I intended to leave it to you in my will."

Struggling to be tactful, she asked, "May I ask . . . what attracted you to this . . . this—"

"It has sentimental significance. My mother was an advocate of celerity. Jumping over candlesticks was part of my early training."

Polly was not fond of teasing. She walked away. "Where's the wall hanging?"

Qwilleran switched on the living room

lights, spotlighting the oversized red-breasted birds.

She gasped. "Did you choose it?"

"I can't take credit. Fran picked it out, and I happen to like her taste. It's perfect scale for the room. Much needed touch of color. Dynamic design. Do you like it?"

"I think it's repulsive!" she said vehemently. "That worm! It's like a snake!"

"It's in proportion to the robins and the—" he began.

"How can you ask your guests to sit here, enjoying a drink while those obscenely fat robins are torturing a helpless fellow creature? Ugh!" She turned on her heel and headed for the door.

"I'll walk you home," he offered.

"That won't be necessary! What did Robert Graves say? *Murderous robin with breast aglow!*" She slammed the door.

Qwilleran looked at Koko, who had been auditing the conversation. "Women!" he said.

Koko squeezed his eyes.

The next morning, about eight-thirty, Qwilleran was thinking about coffee, and the cats were thinking about breakfast, and Polly (he knew) would be thinking about driving to work. At that moment the doorbell rang.

Through the sidelight he could see her on the doorstep. He thought, She's here to make up after her tantrum last night, in which case, I'll apologize for teasing her. Opening the door, he said graciously, "Good morning! What an unexpected pleasure!"

She looked alarmingly wide-eyed. "Qwill! I've just had a strange phone call!"

"Come in!" he said, putting a hand to his unshaved jaw.

She stepped into the foyer. "I'm on my way to work, but I simply had to tell you!"

"Sit down. Who called you?"

She took one of the two pull-up chairs in the foyer, perching on the front edge of the seat. "Mrs. Stebbins, Maggie's housekeeper! She reported for work this morning and found the house empty. No Maggie . . . no cats! Her bed hadn't been slept in; her luggage was gone; and a lot of her clothing was gone. She was bewildered!"

"I'm bewildered, too," he said.

"And then she went into the kitchen and found an envelope containing a month's wages and instructions to empty the refrigerator, take away the fresh flowers, and tell Mrs. Duncan she'd miss the board meeting. What do you make out of that, Qwill?"

He hesitated only a moment. "She's eloping with Henry."

"I doubt it. She values her independence, and Henry doesn't like cats."

"What did she do with them? Traveling with five cats is somewhat of a problem."

"She'd never send them back to the animal shelter, but she might leave them with the new boarding kennel in Kennebeck."

Qwilleran said, "Last night Henry mentioned that he'd sold his house and was living at the Mackintosh Inn until his new place is ready. Let me phone to see if he's checked out. It'll take only a minute."

He returned from the phone with the information that Henry Zoller had checked out last evening, leaving no forwarding instructions. "It appears he drives a Land Rover; that's what was parked next to Maggie's car last night. If it were a Missing Persons case, the police could put a check on it, but it's really none of our business, is it?"

"Yow-ow-ow!" was Koko's contribution to the discussion.

Polly said, "He wants me to get out and go to work."

While preparing the cats' breakfast, Qwilleran asked himself: Why did Zoller choose to have dinner at Maggie's last night instead of attending the reception for the dermatologists at the country club— where he was president? . . . Why did he show no interest in the loss of the bookstore or the arrival of a rare-book dealer selling ten-thousand-dollar books? According to Polly, he had given generously to the library in the past, but only because Maggie twisted his arm. . . . And why was there no discussion of the mayoral race? Probably because Amanda was Maggie's longtime friend and Mayor Blythe was Zoller's golf buddy. . . . And why had they found it appropriate to sneak away like a pair of juvenile lovebirds? Maggie might enjoy fooling her friends, but there was no nonsense about Henry Zoller. . . . And did they drive to Florida in his Land Rover, or fly? And if they went by plane, did they fly from the Moose County or Lockmaster airport?

Qwilleran's final question was: Why do I bother my head about these two characters? I'm turning into a genuine Pickax busybody! Still, he was haunted by unanswered questions.

It was Friday, and he met his noon deadline for the "Qwill Pen" column, grabbed a burger for lunch, and stopped at Amanda's studio to exchange his robin batik. Fran was out making calls.

"What's the matter? Are you squeamish?" Amanda said in her usual brusque manner.

"No, but Polly is, and I aim to keep everyone happy," Qwilleran replied. "Is it cheaper without the worm?"

"We'll deduct fifty cents from your bill."

"I met a friend of yours last night."

"Who?"

"The famous Dr. Zoller."

"He's no friend of mine!"

"We had dinner in Maggie's apartment, and I must compliment you on cramming so much stuff into the parlor without suffocating the guests."

Amanda growled. "I give the customers what they want!"

"Did you ever stand under the chandelier and get a treatment?"

"Did Maggie feed you that hogwash? What else did she feed you?"

"A delicious *bisque l'homard, filet de boeuf,* and *mousse chocolat blanc.*"

"No wonder it's good! Stebbins has been making that for dinner parties for the last ten years!"

The Morghans lived on Pleasant Street, a historic neighborhood in Pickax. Large frame houses in Carpenter Gothic style were lavished with gingerbread trim around porches, doors, windows, and gables, giving the street a festive appearance and enhancing property values.

When Qwilleran rang the old-fashioned jangling doorbell at one o'clock, the door opened promptly and he was confronted by two frisky little dogs and a bright yellow sunflower, four times lifesize. It was on the person of the bright-eyed Misty.

"Nice shirt," he said.

"Batik," she said. "Come in, and wel-

come to the doghouse. . . . Go back!"
she ordered them, and they trotted away.

"Good dogs," Qwilleran said. "What are
their names?"

"Harold and Maude."

"Yorkshire terriers?" They were tiny
things shrouded in long straight hair down
to the floor. Ribbons tied the hair back out
of their large, bright eyes.

"Yes, they were developed two hundred
years ago by Yorkshire miners who wanted
a dog small enough to fit in a pocket—for
killing rats! Now they're just wonderful
companions and full of pep."

Qwilleran said, "I was here when
MacMurchie had the place. He retired from
plumbing and heating and moved to an
apartment."

"Yes, I know. The house has fabulous
plumbing. I believe that's why we bought
it."

"Where's your studio? Let's see where
you work."

He had never seen a batik studio before.
He was familiar with the weaver's loom, the
potter's wheel, the metalsmith's anvil, and
the painter's easel, but . . . *this!* "What

are those large, flat pans?" he asked, turning on his tape recorder.

"Those are vats for the dye baths," she said. "The batik technique is a process of repeated tub dying. Using melted wax, you paint out the areas you don't want to be dyed, and you repeat the process over and over until you have all the colors you want—where you want them."

"Complicated!" he said.

"Fascinating! It takes an understanding of color mixing and overdying." She showed him several squares of fabric like pillow tops, illustrating the development of the design from vat to vat. "I'll use these in my demo at the art center."

Qwilleran said, "Where has this art been all my life?"

"It's been around for centuries, originally in the South Pacific, Asia, and parts of Africa."

"My wall hanging has an allover crackled effect that makes it look antique."

"That happens when the wax cracks in the dye bath. I do it intentionally. Are you enjoying your batik?"

"I must make a confession. In response

to public demand I exchanged the one with worm for the one without worm."

She shrugged. "That's all right. That's why I made two. Will you have coffee?"

They sat in large wicker chairs built close to the floor. He wondered how he would get out when the time came.

"You weren't at the reception last night," Misty said.

"I wasn't invited. How was it?"

"Well . . . you know those affairs." She fluttered her hand. "But they did one nice thing. They invited me to hang some of my batiks in the foyer of the club, and as a result I got a nice commission. I'm not supposed to talk about it, but it's so exciting— and I know you won't blab. They want large hangings of the ten shafthouses!"

"Sensational!" Qwilleran said. "Do you think you'll join the club?"

"Theo's partner will, but we're more interested in the curling club. And the theatre club. We met the Lanspeaks—wonderful people. And a big man in a Scottish kilt who's going to handle the accounting for the clinic. And the mayor—very handsome, but he's had cosmetic surgery. And one poor man must have had a terrible accident; I can tell his whole face has been reconstructed. I can't help it, I have an artist's eye that sees more than it should see. Theo says it's scary. Funny thing, though. All the men at the reception said they liked my artwork, and all the women said they liked my husband.''

When it was time to leave, Harold and Maude appeared to escort Qwilleran to the door, and Misty said, ''Who sings the puppy song on WPKX?''

''Derek Cuttlebrink. It's not his normal voice. He's played many roles for the theatre club.''

''Does he write his own songs?''

''Uh . . . it would appear so.''

''Would he write a song about Harold and Maude and record it? I'd like to give it to Theo for his birthday.''

''Well . . . no harm in asking, but I happen to know he's very busy—attending classes at MCCC and working evenings as maître d' in the Mackintosh Room.''

''I'll work on it,'' Misty said. ''What did you say his name is. *Derek . . . Cuttlebrink*?''

* * *

Having collected inspiration for his next column, Qwilleran turned his attention to unanswered questions. The first led him to Lanspeaks' department store, where he hoped to see Carol or Larry. He found Carol setting up a scarf display in the accessory department.

"Good-looking scarfs," he said. "I'd like to buy one for Polly. What would she like?"

"Well . . . she has that new brown suit, and I have a silk scarf that would give it snap—an oversized houndstooth check in brown and white."

"Sold!"

"You're my favorite customer, Qwill. Gift-wrapped?"

"Please . . . How was the reception last night? I've just interviewed Misty Morghan, and she was quite enthusiastic."

"The Morghans are a lovely couple! We hope to get them into the theatre club."

Qwilleran said casually, "I thought the officers of the club usually attended those affairs, and yet last night I met Henry Zoller having fun at a private dinner party."

Carol lowered her voice. "He resigned the presidency when he left XYZ. I'm afraid there's some bad feeling."

Qwilleran left the store with his purchase and the answer to one question.

His next objective: a piece of apple pie at Lois's Luncheonette, a good source of local information and comfort food. The lunch crowd had left, and Lenny Inchpot was clearing tables. He helped his mother afternoons, attended morning classes at MCCC, and worked the registration desk at the Mackintosh Inn in the evening.

"Too late for the luncheon special!" Lois Inchpot yelled through the kitchen pass-through.

"I'll settle for apple pie and coffee!" Qwilleran shouted in her direction.

Lenny asked, "Will it bug you, Mr. Q, if I sweep up?"

"Not if you split with me any money you find. . . . By the way, congratulations on winning the last race before snow flies."

"Thanks. I did it for Mom. But don't tell her."

"Would she let you sit down and have a cup of coffee with me? Or is she cracking the whip today?"

"Who's talkin' about me behind my back?" came the gruff challenge through the pass-through.

Qwilleran chuckled; Lenny grinned and sat down; and the conversation began:

"Last night I met Dr. Zoller for the first time."

"Nice guy. He's been staying at the Inn. Big tipper."

"I tried to reach him this morning, but he'd checked out."

"Yeah. Funny time to be checking out— eleven-thirty P.M."

"Unless he was catching a plane."

"No flights at that hour. Could've been driving somewhere."

"I believe he drives a Land Rover."

"That's what it says on the register. Not many of those around here."

"Did he look happy? He might have been eloping."

"Nah. He never showed his emotions."

"Lenny! Stop gabbin' and peel some potatoes," came the order from the kitchen.

He jumped to his feet. "Gotta go, or she'll be out here with the rolling pin."

Qwilleran's quest for answers next took him to an establishment new to Moose County—a nationally franchised luxury-class boarding kennel.

The Pet Plaza occupied the former premises of Chet's Barbecue, closed after its owner found himself in bad trouble. Qwilleran assumed that lingering aromas of roasting meat might add to its success as a boarding kennel. For whatever reason, it was said to be a howling success in spite of the high daily rates. That was understandable; Moose County had plenty of affluent families descended from mining tycoons, lumber barons, and early twentieth-century bootleggers. They traveled frequently and had thoroughbred pets who deserved the best.

The plain two-story building of concrete block had been given a tongue-in-cheek facelift. Classic columns, a pediment, and low-relief sculptures of mythical gods and goddesses had been painted on the flat surface. It looked quite grand until one noticed that the robed figures had the heads of cats and dogs.

When Qwilleran walked into the lobby he was met by a young woman in a natty gray pantsuit with silver buttons.

"Lori Bamba!" he said in surprise. "Aren't you supposed to be running a bed-and-breakfast?"

"It was too iffy."

"How's the family?"

"The boys are growing fast; they want their own computers. Nick is doing maintenance engineering, but he'd rather be an innkeeper. I'm concierge here; my job is to keep the guests happy."

"The dogs sound happy," said Qwilleran, cocking an ear to hear a distant symphony of barks, woofs, yelps, and yodels. "What facilities do you offer?"

"The Oak Room for dogs, the Oyster Bar for cats, and the Palm Court for exercise."

"Piano entertainment in the Oak Room?" he asked.

"Where would you like to start?"

In Moose County he was accustomed to seeing collies, German shepherds, coonhounds, and pit bulls. Lori pointed out an Alaskan malamute, a pair of Jack Russells, a Lhasa apso from Tibet, an exuberant Welsh corgi, and an amiable Bouvier from Belgium. They were housed in top-of-the-line cages of various sizes, and those on the outside wall had direct access to the dog run.

In the Oyster Bar the cats had split-level cages with picture windows overlooking a grassy plot. They seemed contented, except for a Siamese who was being shampooed and blow-dried before going home. A Persian was sleeping in his litter pan. Qwilleran spotted an Abyssinian, a Rex, and an Oriental before seeing the five genteel hybrids whose nameplates read: Sarah, Charlotte, Carrie, Flora, and Louisa May—Maggie's "ladies."

"Are these all from one family?" he asked innocently.

"Yes. They came in yesterday and will be staying for a month."

Lori went on talking, and the recorder went on recording: "Some cats are on special diets. . . . Some are here for a get-acquainted visit before being left for two weeks or more. . . . Some bring their own security blankets from home. . . . Our staff is hardworking, observant, and loving. . . . There is a waiting list for employment here."

"How do I get on the list?" Qwilleran asked, but his mind was on Maggie, who had lied when she said her ladies had retired early to their boudoir upstairs. He had noticed that there were no cat hairs on her black velvet dress.

nine

Hanging anything on a wall was not one of Qwilleran's talents, but suddenly the chimney breast looked obscenely nude without its three- by four-foot batik. He unrolled the new one, without worm, and brought a stepladder from the basement. The mantel was high; the hanging seemed enormous; the ladder was wobbly; and the two assistants were incompetents who wanted only to inspect the ladder.

"Get away!" he said. "Your job is to stand back and tell me if it's level."

As soon as he reached the fourth step, the phone rang.

"Yow!" said Koko.

"Let it ring."

"YOW!"

"They can leave a message."

"Yow-ow-ow!"

Qwilleran thought, It could be important! It could be urgent! He lobbed the batik at the hook in the wall as if shooting a basket from mid-court, and jumped off the ladder. His helpers scattered.

It was only Susan Exbridge. "Darling! I have something for you, and I'll drop it off on my way home from work, if you'll be there about five-thirty. It's the natal chart—for your friend Ronald."

"I was hoping it would be a half-gallon of chocolate ice cream. Will you come in for a drink?"

He climbed up and straightened the hanging, returned the ladder to the basement, tidied the coffee table, and checked his martini ingredients. Plenty of gin, three kinds of olives, no dry vermouth. Nevertheless, he was famous for his fourteen-to-one mix, and Susan wouldn't notice if he served it fourteen-to-zero.

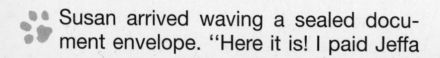 Susan arrived waving a sealed document envelope. "Here it is! I paid Jeffa

for it, so you can write a check payable to me, and your anonymity will be secure."

She flung herself onto the sofa with a sigh. "I had a hard day at the cash register! Mind if I take off my shoes? This rug is positively degenerate! . . . Is that one of the batty batiks everyone's talking about? The robin should be pulling a worm out of the lawn."

"I had one like that," Qwilleran said, "but public outrage forced me to exchange it for the wormless version."

"It isn't quite level."

"We had a minor earthquake today. Nothing serious." He served his guest a martini and himself some white grape juice in a martini glass.

She took a sip. "Superb! You're wasting your time as a journalist, Qwill. You should be a bartender."

"I've considered switching. Bartending pays better."

"Oh! . . . You have one of those martini pitchers from a French liner! Where did you get it?"

"It was a gift."

"Maggie has one just like it."

"It came from a large ship. They had two."

She ignored his arch remark. "Let me know if you ever want to sell it."

Qwilleran asked, "Did you see your ex-husband's letter to the editor—in praise of shafthouses?"

"I did! And was that ever a joke! He's always hated those shafthouses! Either he's cracking up or falling in love again. His second wife has filed for divorce, you know, and now he'll have to write two big alimony checks."

"Will he attend Amanda's rally Sunday?"

"Not likely. He and the mayor will be having their last golf game before snow flies. The astrologer will be there, though, and you must meet her! She has a phenomenal mind for mathematics and a degree in accounting. Astrology is her hobby." Susan drained her glass. "Will you excuse me? I have to dress for dinner."

He said, "I'll let you know, Susan, what I think about my horoscope."

"Please, darling! We call it a natal chart."

"I stand corrected."

On the way out she noticed the glove

box in the foyer. "Where did you find that? It's old but not antique—probably 1920s."

"It was a gift, and it's not for sale."

Qwilleran sprawled in a deep-cushioned chair and propped his feet on an ottoman, as he proceeded to read about himself. The chart consisted of two dozen pages in a plastic binder, with a frontispiece of a twelve-spoked wheel filled with arcane symbols and mathematical notations. First, it told him he was a Gemini.

You are constantly investigating, asking questions, communicating, wanting to know "why?" You have a talent for writing and speaking.

Qwilleran thought, Mildred would fall for this stuff. But how do they do it? Then came a description of his past, leaving him somewhat flabbergasted.

You have been deprived of one parent but doubly fortunate in the one remaining. Your early career involved much traveling. . . . An early marriage has been short-lived. . . . Material possessions come late in life. . . . A previous acquaintance comes back into your life, bringing great benefits.

"Incredible!" he said aloud. "That's Fanny Klingenschoen!"

Physically, your weakness is in your knees.

That had been true until he moved to Moose County and started walking and biking.

Family life passes you by, but animals are a great comfort.

"This is too much!" he protested.

Other persons perceive you as wise, generous, helpful, and trustworthy.

"Yow!" came a clarion comment from another part of the condo.

It was all convincing and comforting to his ego, but it overlooked one of his traits: skepticism. It stopped him from accepting his "natal chart" without a quibble. Before he could marshal his objections, however, Derek Cuttlebrink called. "Hi, Mr. Q! Are you going to Amanda's rally?"

"I wouldn't miss it!"

"They want me to take my guitar."

"Not to play the puppy song, I hope."

"They thought I could write a campaign song," Derek said hesitantly. "Could you help me out?"

It was Qwilleran's turn to hesitate. "Does

anyone suspect I was responsible for the puppy song?"

"Not even Elizabeth."

"If it ever gets out that I'm your under-ground lyricist, I'll have your guitar confis-cated—and your driver's license revoked!" Then he thought, Her campaign slogan will fit "She'll Be Comin' Round the Mountain."

Derek said, "You wouldn't have to pull any punches. She's tough. Everybody knows she's been to rehab. If she hadn't dried out, she wouldn't be challenging hiz-zoner."

"Tell you what, Derek. Get me a reserva-tion tomorrow night—for two—and when you seat us, I'll slip you a folded piece of paper."

"Gee thanks, Mr. Q. I know it's short no-tice—"

"That's the best kind."

Polly was having a dinner meeting with her board of directors, so Qwilleran thawed something for his dinner and was at work on Amanda's battle hymn when Koko staged his someone's-coming tizzy. He was as good as an electronic sensor.

Qwilleran went outdoors in time to find Wetherby Goode driving home in his van.

He called out, "How's everything on the fire watch, Joe?"

"Not many alerts. I'm on standby. I go out if there's a cancellation. . . . Say, I have a question to ask. You probably hear a lot of jokes. I heard a good one the other day about a pastor who thought his bicycle had been stolen, but—"

"You've forgotten the punch line," Qwilleran guessed.

"I remember the punch line. I've forgotten the joke. I thought you might know it."

"Try me!"

"Then I remembered where I'd left my bicycle." Seeing the blank look on his friend's face, Wetherby said, "If you hear it, call me at any hour of the day or night. . . . Hey, your phone's ringing."

"Where were you? Asleep?" Arch Riker asked when Qwilleran came to the phone.

"Who's calling? Big Brother?"

"If you're not busy, I'd like to walk over there and discuss something."

Qwilleran said, "I'll have to ask the boss. He's right here, sitting on the desk. . . .

Koko, your uncle Arch wants to come over for a while."

"Yow!" said Koko, reacting to a friendly poke in the ribs.

"He says it's okay, but he wants the lights out at eleven."

Riker arrived with a manila envelope, which he threw on the coffee table. "Where'd you get the glass pitcher?" he asked. "Are those real apples? Do you know that thing over the mantel is crooked?"

"That 'thing' is a batik, and it's more dynamic when hung crooked."

Riker looked at the deep-pile rug. "Is it safe to step on it? I don't want to turn my ankle." He stepped carefully across it and sank into the deep-cushioned contemporary sofa. "I'd hate to have to get out of this mantrap if there's fire."

Qwilleran served him a glass of cider.

"A kachug of rum wouldn't hurt it, pal."

"Okay, what's on your mind, Arch?"

"You saw Don Exbridge's Pollyanna letter in Monday's paper. What was your reaction?"

"A—he can't be sincere, and B—what's his motive?"

"Well, since then, there's been a back-lash. We've had a dozen letters in opposition. They'll run Monday and create controversy. I wanted you to have a preview and give an opinion." He drew proofs from the manila envelope and handed them over. "The originals were written on fancy stationery, lined sheets from school notebooks, copy paper, and one greeting card left over from Easter."

Qwilleran scanned them, frequently touching his moustache. The letters were signed with names he did not recognize and came from the larger towns in the county.

Why the big fuss about shaft-houses? They're just ugly old shacks, and the fences with barbed wire on top look like concentration camps waiting for another war. My advice is—fill in the mineshafts, chop up the shaft-houses for firewood, and give us some family parks with playground equipment, picnic tables and a few shade trees. And don't forget restrooms. . . .

All that hoopla about shafthouses, and Pickax is in bad need of cemetery space. We honor the early settlers who died a hundred years ago and don't provide burial space for today's loved ones. . . .

Moose County has never had a zoo. Let's close up one of the mines and have a petting zoo where kids can see baby goats and lambs, calves and colts, and little piglets. It would be fun for the whole family, and the kids would learn something. . . .

All that space wasted on forests and minesites, and some of us don't have a place to live. Give us mobile home parks. . . .

Where the old mines are now would make wonderful vegetable gardens for poor families who don't have enough space to plant a turnip. Or turn the land over to the schools and let the kids raise vegetables, sell them, and use the money for band instruments and athletic equipment. . . .

Who wants to drive around looking at dumb shafthouses? Sports and recreation—that's the ticket. Every community should have a softball diamond and a soccer field. Put the minesites to work. . . .

Qwilleran huffed into his moustache. "They were all composed by the same person and copied by different individuals. There are little clues in the sentence structure and vocabulary."

"You're probably right," Arch said. "There were no return addresses on the envelopes—not one of them! We checked signatures in the phone book, and none was listed. Not one, mind you."

Qwilleran chuckled. "Remember, Arch, when we were teens and crazy about baseball? A Chicago Cubs catcher told a sportswriter he never received fan mail; pitchers and sluggers got it all. So I wrote him eight letters, supposedly from a truck driver, an old man, a young girl, and so forth."

"You composed them, and we copied them in different handwriting. My grandfather copied the old man's letter."

"And the catcher told the sportswriter he'd suddenly received a bushel of mail, but I think it was only our eight."

"We felt we'd done a good deed," Arch said. "We'll consult our lawyer about these. . . . Meanwhile remember the geologist who phoned to tell us about subterranean fires? We checked his credentials before quoting him. But he was a fraud. The real geologist wrote us a letter, which we've turned over to our attorney. . . . *There's always something!*"

"Especially at the *Something,*" Qwilleran said sympathetically.

There was something more that night. Sometime after midnight, as Qwilleran was trying to read himself to sleep, the stillness was broken by a tortured wail ending in a shriek. He ran into the cats' room and found Koko sitting on the TV and howling at the ceiling. It meant bad news. And it meant bad news close to home.

Qwilleran called the night desk at the *Something.* "Any trouble on the police beat?"

"We don't know the details, but there's

been a shooting. We don't know who, where, or if it's fatal."

Koko knew it was fatal.

The night editor added, "I believe it was a volunteer."

With a shudder Qwilleran thought of Wetherby, always taking a patrol if another driver had to cancel. They had talked a few hours before. . . . Then he heard the toilet flush next door, and for the first time he gave thanks instead of cursing the thin walls.

ten

Qwilleran slept poorly as the list of volunteers reeled through his mind. Civic leaders like Ernie Kemple and Larry Lanspeak were on standby, night or day. Among the regulars were Dwight Somers, the McBee brothers, Gordie Shaw, Bob the barber, Albert the dry cleaner, Lenny Inchpot, many staffers at the *Something,* city council members, and more. There were women who drove patrols, but they were excluded from nighttime shifts. Even Grandma Toodle, the manager of the supermarket, was a ride-along with her grandson.

Rising early and feeding the Siamese

mechanically, he listened for a radio bulletin. The first news from WPKX was: "A citizen on fire-watch patrol was killed early this morning by a gunman attempting to burn the Big B shafthouse. The victim's name has not been released." The station had the good taste to follow the announcement with *Loch Lomond* and not the Pickax puppy song, which had become their virtual signature.

Qwilleran could imagine the telephone lines sizzling as relatives and friends phoned each other frantically to ask who was on patrol last night. As he brooded over cup after cup of coffee, the Siamese sensed the troubled atmosphere and sat quietly nearby instead of seeking out patches of sunlight for their own enjoyment. Suddenly Koko ran to the radio, and a few moments later the WPKX announcer broke into the music with this news:

"Ralph Abbey of Chipmunk, a volunteer fire-watcher, was killed early this morning at the Big B minesite while reporting to the sheriff's hotline on his cellular phone. He was reporting trespassing and vandalism when the operator heard a shot. The rescue squad was alerted, and firefighters were already on the way. Flames creeping toward the shafthouse were extinguished, but the victim was pronounced dead at the scene."

Qwilleran's phone began to ring, and he listened to comments for the next half hour:

Wetherby Goode said, "Hey, Qwill, do you realize that might have happened to you and me? The irony of it is that Abbey had racked up more volunteer hours than anyone else—patrolling every day, sometimes twice in twenty-four hours."

Polly said, "I knew him when he was a high school student bringing his homework assignments to the library. He was more of an athletic type than a scholarly one, but he was conscientious."

Then Fran Brodie called in a highly emotional state. "Qwill! That fellow who was killed! He was Ruff, my installer! The one who hung your batik! Such a nice young man! Such a good worker! We encouraged him to take classes at MCCC. So young! Only twenty-two! And what will happen now? He was supporting his mother and three younger sisters. His father died of diabetes. . . . And to think that it happened because he was doing a community service! The county should set up a trust to take care of the family. Do you think the K Fund would help?"

"Definitely! Talk to G. Allen Barter."

After that, Qwilleran went downtown to observe and listen. Crowds had turned out of their homes; friends were commiserating with friends, and strangers were talking to strangers. There was a wreath on the door at Amanda's studio, and a sign stated "CLOSED until Tuesday—in mourning for our valued colleague, Ruff Abbey."

At the post office, patrons bought stamps but lingered to talk, and it was surprising what they found to say to each other.

"He didn't like to be called Ralph."

"His family goes to our church. We're going to have a hymn-sing to raise money for them."

"He was a football hero in high school."

"He never said much, but he had opinions."

"He bagged an eight-point buck last year in huntin' season. Got his picture in the paper."

"His mother does sewing for people in her home, but she doesn't make much."

"He hung my draperies and did an expert job."

"The county should give him an official funeral."

"I used to date him; he was a real sweet guy."

In the background were the murals, showing the ancestors of these people, working in the mines, tilling fields with hand plows, driving oxcarts, spinning yarn from sheep's wool.

One elderly gentleman said, "You're Mr. Q, aren't you? When I don't like the way things are going, I come in here and see how my ancestors lived."

Qwilleran went to the police station to see Brodie, but the chief was attending a summit meeting at the courthouse. Roger MacGillivray was there, waiting for a newsbreak. "It's getting the whole front page Monday."

"Any chance the Fire Watch will be discontinued?"

"No way! The sheriff took a telephone poll of volunteers this morning, and the vote was unanimous to continue. It won't be long before snow flies, and the problem will be over."

Qwilleran asked, "Feel like lunch? I'm buying. We could go to Rennie's."

The Mackintosh Inn's colorful coffee shop was still new enough to be a special attraction.

They ordered Reuben sandwiches, and Roger said, "Ruff was in my history classes when I was teaching. All-right guy!"

"Do you know exactly what happened last night?"

"Well, he was on patrol midnight to three and saw something irregular at the Big B Mine—a car parked in the side lane and a brushfire creeping toward the shafthouse. Instead of reporting it from the highway, he drove into the lane behind the car, apparently to get the license number. That's where he was found, behind the wheel, but he'd already reported the fire and the number on the tag. The hotline operator heard the shot on the phone and heard it drop. Two shots were heard. Fire and police vehicles were already on the way. The suspect got away by driving around the back of the minesite."

Both then gulped their sandwiches in silence. Then Qwilleran said, "The suspect must have been a local, if he knew about the perimeter road."

"His car had an out-of-state plate. The state and local police are having a summit meeting at the courthouse. . . . which reminds me: I've got to get back on my beat. Thanks for lunch, Qwill."

Qwilleran sat for a while, thinking about the shooting and lingering over a slice of coconut cream pie, too sweet for his taste.

Then Susan Exbridge walked past his table and asked him conspiratorially, "What—do you—think about it?"

He rose politely. "Too sweet. They have a new pastry chef."

"Please sit down," she murmured. "I was referring to Ronald's natal chart."

He continued to stand. "Ronald sends his compliments to Mrs. Young."

"Please sit down, Qwill," she said firmly.

"I don't want to sit down!" he replied testily. "I want to pay for my lunch and get out of here and go home to my cats."

"Oh!" she said in surprise.

"Are you coming in or going out?"

"I've come to have lunch with two of my customers." She spoke with unusual meekness.

"Then enjoy your lunch, and don't order the pie."

He signed the tab at the cash register, and the cashier said, "I heard that, Mr. Q. It was really funny."

"It's an old comic routine," he explained. "I couldn't resist. I like to tease Mrs. Exbridge once in a while. . . . I'll buy lunch for her party. Put it on my tab."

"What a pleasant surprise!" Polly said when she discovered they were dining at the Mackintosh Room. "I hear it's impossible to get a reservation on Saturday night."

"It helps if your middle name is Mackintosh."

"Did you hear anything about the commotion last night, around midnight?"

"What kind of commotion?"

"In Kirt's condo. I thought Wetherby might have heard it and mentioned it."

"Wetherby was probably off on one of his mysterious weekends in Horseradish. What was the commotion?"

"Kirt was having a terrible row with another man. I looked out the bedroom window, but there was no car in the visitors' slot."

"Have you talked to him lately?" Qwilleran asked.

"No, I was beginning to feel uncomfortable with him. He mistook my small-town neighborliness for something else. Have you talked with him?"

"Not since Koko scared him out of his wits with a pot of geraniums."

When they arrived at the Mackintosh Room, the maître d' showed them to the best table in the house, and Qwilleran slipped him a little something.

"May we bring you Scotch eggs—with our compliments?" Derek asked.

The traditional appetizer was a whole hard-cooked egg encased in well-flavored sausage meat—served in lengthwise quarters with mustard and a garnish.

"I could live on these," Qwilleran told Polly. "Are you going to eat all of yours?"

"Of course! Is my name Duncan? What did you do today?"

Be careful, he told himself; don't mention Susan and the natal chart; don't mention Amanda's campaign song. Even Ronald Frobnitz was a secret.

"Nothing much," he said. "Just moseyed around downtown."

"Mosey! That's the first time I've heard you use that word. I must admit it sounds like what it means."

They could talk for hours about words. There was a game they played at dinner. The word "delicious" was out of bounds. On this occasion the eggs were robust, the grilled salmon was succulent, the salad had verve, Polly's blackberry cobbler had zest, and Qwilleran's seven-layer chocolate cake had a certain nobility.

"Have you had any more crazy dreams?" she asked.

"Yes, I dreamed that Koko and Yum Yum gave a party for Brutus and Catta. And they invited Toulouse and Jet Stream because a successful party always has more male guests than female guests."

Between her laughter she said, "I don't know anyone who dreams as fancifully and creatively as you do!"

The truth was that he invented dreams to amuse her; there were so many things they could not discuss, despite their intimacy: his hunches that began as twitches in his moustache; Koko's remarkable intuition;

the unofficial investigations that interested both cat and man. Polly did not understand and would not believe. Arch Riker, his life-long friend, was the same way, saying, "It's none of your business. Don't waste your time."

Whether Qwilleran admitted it or not, there was a kind of loneliness in his life. About the cats he would say, "They're all the family I've got." There was his alias, Ronald Frobnitz, of course. But if I ever start conversing with him, Qwilleran told himself, I'm sick!

On Sunday afternoon the residents of Indian Village swarmed out of their condos on River Road and apartments on Woodland Trail and converged on the club-house for the rally. Carloads of Amanda's supporters also arrived from Pickax.

The event was held in the great hall, which had the feeling of a ski lodge, with its imposing stone fireplace, high ceiling criss-crossed with log rafters, and bright red car-pet. For the occasion a large banner with the candidate's slogan spanned the fire-place wall.

It was a well-dressed crowd. There were no jeans, T-shirts, or running shoes.

Qwilleran and Polly had walked over with the Rikers. Just inside the door Hixie Rice and Dwight Somers were selling large lapel buttons—yellow, with Amanda's frizzy-haired caricature and her campaign slogan. She needed no financial support and stipulated that proceeds should go to the Ruff Abbey Trust. Everyone was wearing a button, and a large glass apothecary jar was filling with personal checks and currency of large denomination.

Amanda herself was not there. She would make an entrance at a dramatic moment. Meanwhile, Wetherby Goode was at the piano, playing show tunes, ballads, and a little Strauss. The crowd was circulating, drinking wine punch or fruit punch, and wondering why Maggie Sprenkle was not there; she and Amanda were longtime friends.

Elizabeth Hart, an heiress from Down Below who had discovered Moose County and Derek Cuttlebrink at the same time, said to Qwilleran, "I'm so glad my rya rug went to you. I inherited it from my father; he had such good taste. Someone was bidding against you, but you topped him at the last minute."

"I'm glad to know its provenance," he said. "If we find any diamond rings in the deep pile, we'll know where to return them."

Ernie Kemple, majordomo of the Citizens' Fire Watch, was there with some of his Pleasant Street neighbors: Theo and Misty Morghan, and Burgess Campbell with Alexander, his guide dog.

Whannell MacWhannell was there with an attractive middle-aged woman who wore her dark hair drawn back into a chignon. Polly whispered, "I wonder who she is? Her hair is a little too dark for her age. Mac's wife is very ill, you know. She requires round-the-clock care."

Most of the women were wearing maroon or grape or burgundy, proclaimed the colors of choice for that particular season. "Precisely why I bought a brown suit," Polly said. "I love my houndstooth scarf, Qwill. You have such good taste!"

Gradually they moved over to the vicinity of Big Mac and his new friend. Introductions were made.

MacWhannell said, "Mrs. Young is from

Baltimore. She's joining our firm after the first of the year. She's a certified accountant."

Qwilleran said, "From Baltimore to Pickax is a giant step—forward, I hope."

"I think so," she said. "My son lives here and speaks highly of it. You probably know him. Cass Young."

So this was Jeffa Young, astrologer. Little did she know he was the talented, generous, trustworthy Gemini whose life she had just charted.

The music stopped abruptly to grab everyone's attention, before Wetherby swung into the old Al Jolson hit "Mandy." The big doors opened, and Amanda entered, followed by her bodyguard, Susan Exbridge. Amid applause the candidate marched to the fireplace and faced the crowd. She was wearing a tan gabardine shirtdress with four pockets. All one could say for it was that it was neat and clean. Her hair still looked uncombed, and her face wore a scowl of grim determination.

She waited until the music and applause ended and then said, "I have no intention of making a long speech." She paused for laughter; Mayor Blythe was noted for his boring oratory. "If elected, I will pursue issues to a conclusion instead of tabling them for three years." More laughter. The reference was obvious. "And I guarantee the city hall roof will not leak." This brought whoops of mirth from listeners who knew how to put two and two together.

Immediately Derek Cuttlebrink appeared by her side with his guitar and played her campaign song to the tune of "She'll Be Comin' Round the Mountain When She Comes."

We'd rather have Amanda run our city!
She isn't very sweet or very pretty
But she always sticks to biz
And tells it like it is!
And she's not afraid to face the
nitty-gritty.

He strummed a few chords and flashed the smile that always made his groupies howl. The audience shouted for more.

She'd rather wear a helmet than a
crown.
She never reads the lawbooks upside-down.

She's got a lot of clout
And hey! She finally dried out!
We'd rather have Amanda run our
    town.

The audience exploded with cheers and laughter, and even Amanda managed a faint smile.

Qwilleran said, "If elected, she should appoint Derek as court jester."

"Do you think he wrote that himself?" Mildred asked dubiously.

"It sounds more like Hixie Rice," Polly said. "What do you think, Qwill?"

"It could have been Burgess Campbell. He has a sense of humor."

"Or Alexander," said Arch.

A crowd was gathering around the apothecary jar. Anyone who dropped a dollar bill into the jar would receive a photocopy of the lyrics. Dwight Somers had a portable copier and was cranking them out as fast as he could. Some enthusiasts wanted five or ten copies, and the Ruff Abbey Fund grew accordingly.

As Qwilleran and Polly walked home, she said, "How Maggie would have loved this turnout for Amanda! Why do you suppose they left so suddenly? And why did Maggie have us to dinner without mentioning a word about their plans? It's all very strange to me."

Qwilleran said, "Her cats were already lodged at the Pet Plaza, so she fibbed when she said they were upstairs, sleeping."

"How do you know they're there?" she asked sharply.

"I'm writing a column on the facility, and there they were!"

eleven

The day after the rally, when rain would have been appreciated by the parched county, another morning sun flooded Qwilleran's living room through the large glass areas overlooking the riverbank. Where was the Big One? Water was being rationed. Farmers worried about their flocks and herds. Wetherby Goode talked about going into hiding if the Big One continued to stall over Canada.

When Qwilleran opened his bedroom door and stepped out onto the balcony, he looked down at a dazzling light on the coffee table—enough to alarm him for a moment until he realized it was the French pitcher, reflecting and multiplying the sun's rays. It was a remarkable example of optic lead crystal, chunky and heavy; he estimated it weighed five pounds, empty. Nine deep vertical cuts faceted the spherical base, which was topped with a narrow neck, a perfect pouring spout, and a gracefully well-balanced handle. Even without sunlight the crystal had a life of its own, playing optic tricks with interior shapes and shadows. Koko recognized it as something special and tried to get his sleek head into the pitcher's neck.

"No!" Qwilleran shouted, and the cat withdrew quickly.

"You guys missed a good party yesterday," he told the cats as he was preparing their food. "There was a nice dog there— quiet, intelligent, well-mannered. Your kind of dog. His name was Alexander."

As if some kind of mental telepathy were at work, the phone rang at that moment, and Burgess Campbell was on the line. "I was just talking about Alexander," Qwilleran said. "How did he like the rally yesterday?"

"He takes everything in his stride," Burgess said. "We could all take lessons from Alexander. . . . Why I'm calling, Qwill—Ernie was telling us about your book, *Short & Tall Tales,* and I wondered if you had room for one more."

"Yes, if it has a legendary quality and a Moose County connection."

"I think it qualifies. My father used to tell about this feed-and-seed supplier in Brrr Township in the 1920s. He called it Phineas Ford's Fabulous Collection."

"Are there any Fords still around? I haven't run into that name."

"Dad said the last ones went Down Below during World War Two, to work in the defense industry. If you're interested, I could dictate it to my computer and mail you a printout. Then you can edit it as you see fit."

"Sounds good to me!" Qwilleran said.

Ruff Abbey was given a hero's funeral—on Monday, not Tuesday, because of the threat of the Big One. The service was held in the high school auditorium because so many mourners wanted to attend. Burial was in Sawdust City because the Mudville Curlers insisted.

After the service Qwilleran was cashing a check in the bank when he bumped into someone and said, "Sorry."

The other man said, "Sorry," and then looked up. "Qwill!"

"Ernie! If I'd known it was you, I'd have bumped harder!"

"Story of my life." He lowered his booming voice to a mutter. "Gotta couple of minutes? If we could sit down somewhere and spread this thing out . . ." There was a roll of drafting paper under his arm.

Qwilleran used his influence, and they went into a small conference room.

Ernie Kemple, former insurance agent and enthusiastic volunteer, was not in his usual jovial mood. In the last year he had surmounted family problems and carried on with bravado, throwing himself into community service.

But now he looked discouraged as he unrolled a large drawing of a floor plan. "Did you hear about my idea for an antique village?"

"Sketchily. Fill me in. It sounds interesting."

"The idea was flying high. . . . and then the wings fell off. I suppose you know that Otto's Tasty Eats went out of business."

"Good riddance!"

"Yeah . . . well . . . His building was for sale by owner, and I thought it would be perfect for an antiques cooperative, where dealers rent spaces and take turns minding the store."

Qwilleran asked, "Would this area have enough dealers to make it work?"

"Oh, sure! Collectors all over the county are selling from their barns and basements, and they'd welcome the opportunity to 'go pro,' you know, without a big investment. Also, dealers in surrounding counties could have a branch in Pickax and cash in on the tourist trade. I'd have exhibit booths around the walls of the main floor and balcony, and have a courtyard in the middle for serving lunches and snacks. The K Fund was standing by, ready to give me a low-interest business loan. . . . and then I made Otto an offer for the building, and crash! He said he was planning a business venture of his own!"

Qwilleran said, "Sounds as if he's stealing your idea! Would the dealers tell you if they've been approached by another promoter?"

"What good would it do? He's got the building, and it's perfect for an antique mall operation. It's downtown. It has parking in the municipal lot. It's in the traffic hub." Kemple started to tear up the plans.

"Not so fast, Ernie! Wait and see what happens. Success breeds success, and you've done a great job with the Fire Watch—"

"Yes, but the shooting—!"

"It's a tribute to you. . . . and Ruff . . . and all the other volunteers that the Fire Watch will be continued till snow flies. It could have been worse—much worse—if he hadn't put his call through to the hotline when he did."

"I wonder if they'll ever find the killer," Kemple said.

Qwilleran drew a heavy hand over his moustache. He had a hunch they would.

Qwilleran drove home with a desire for a large dish of ice cream to comfort his distress over Kemple's plight. On the bright side, Otto might be opening a roller rink, disco hall, video parlor, or basketball arena. Then Ernie could have his antique village in a building designed for the purpose—perhaps a Swiss chalet like the curling club—out in the country!

Arriving at Indian Village he stopped at the gatehouse for mail and was unlocking his mailbox when he caught a woman staring at his moustache. He recognized her hairdo.

"Mrs. Young! We met at the rally yesterday! I'm Jim Qwilleran. I didn't know you're a villager."

"I have a unit between Amanda Goodwinter and Susan Exbridge," she said. "I feel like an out-of-town pygmy between two local giants."

"May I carry that package to your car for you?"

"I'm walking."

"Then let me drop you at your condo."

On the brief ride to River Road she said, "I didn't get a chance to compliment you on your column, Mr. Qwilleran."

"Qwill, please."

"Then you must call me Jeffa."

"MacWhannell & Shaw will be pleased to

have your help during the tax rush, Jeffa. Qualified accountants don't grow on trees in Moose County."

She invited him in for a drink, and he accepted, mindful that he was on thin ice. This woman knew all about his life—past, present, and future—but was unaware of it.

"Soon," he said, "you'll be receiving invitations to Last Drink parties—meaning the last drink before snow flies—after which you may be snowbound for up to a week. Have plenty of crossword puzzles on hand."

"I always have my planetary calculations to work on," she said. "My sideline is astrology."

"Is that so?" he exclaimed, feigning surprise and expressing admiration.

"It's a fascinating science—so exact! It's possible to chart an individual's whole lifetime of planetary influences, given the time and place of birth. It's the calculation that's absorbing. It can be done faster by computer, but I find the traditional method—with mathematics—more enjoyable. What is needed is the exact hour and minute of birth, taking into consideration time zones and standard or daylight time. Also needed is the latitude and longitude of the birth-place, in degrees and minutes."

Soon, Qwilleran felt, she would ask if he knew his birth data. To deflect her train of thought he asked, "Have you charted the lives of your family? And do they check out as the years go by?"

"As a matter of fact, that's why I'm here," she said. "My son is facing a chal-lenge, and I thought my motherly presence might give him moral support if nothing else."

She was eager to talk about her family, and he listened with sympathetic nods and murmurs.

"You probably know my son as Caspar, named after a Revolutionary War hero, but we call him Cass. My father's name was Jefferson, which explains mine. When my husband died, Cass urged me to come here. My daughter in Idaho wanted me to go there. I have grandchildren in Coeur d'Alene, a lovely resort town in the north-west part of the state. It was named by early French explorers. . . . but it was Cass's challenge that brought me here. You know, of course, that he handled the construction for XYZ Enterprises. Even when he was a tot, I knew he was born to build. He went on to learn his craft in the East, then established himself here because of the hunting and winter sports. When a local developer took him in as a partner, Cass was in his element."

"Yes, when I came here, XYZ was doing schools, medical buildings, housing—everything. It was the most prestigious firm in the county—perhaps three counties."

"There was one thing wrong," Jeffa said, "and you probably know what it was. The senior partner was greedy; he wanted to build fast and cut corners. Cass knew how to build with integrity, but he was overruled."

Qwilleran was entranced by her soft Baltimore accent, but he was surprised to hear her relating details of family affairs. He thought, She's lonely. . . . in a strange environment . . . in need of someone to talk to. Had no one explained the dangers, large and small, of talking too much in a small town? No doubt it was Qwilleran's sympathetic mien that encouraged her; he also had a compulsion—as a journalist and a Gemini—to hear it all.

He said, "It was an unfortunate situation. Why did Cass compromise? Why didn't he quit?"

"Well, first, he was making very good money. And there was the outdoor life that meant so much to him. And he was in love with a local woman."

"People have compromised for a lot less."

Abruptly she asked, "Do you know Don Exbridge?"

"I do."

"Is he a friend of yours?"

"Not by a long shot. I've never forgiven him for trying to ruin Breakfast Island. Fortunately, nature had the last word."

"Did you see the item in the paper about XYZ? They've dissolved, and Cass is striking out on his own as a house builder. . . . The challenge will be, I think, overcoming his past reputation as a builder of leaky roofs."

Qwilleran said, "Frank Lloyd Wright had the same image but came out smelling like a rose. Cass needs to meet Dwight

Somers, an expert at building favorable images. And it wouldn't hurt in a community like this, if Cass married that woman of his and started a family."

Jeffa hesitated. "She's married. . . . She's currently married to Don Exbridge."

Qwilleran stood up. "Then tell your son, Jeffa, that he really needs Dwight Somers. . . . Thanks for the refreshments. I've enjoyed the chat. I hope you're very happy here. Let me know if there's anything I can do."

Arriving home he found a recorded message from Polly, calling from the library: "Come over at six o'clock if you'd like a surprise."

He envisioned beef stew or fried chicken from a library volunteer; they often brought their beloved director home-cooked food, knowing she had little time to cook. He showered and dressed, wearing the royal blue madras shirt that she liked and the Scottish scent she had brought him from Canada.

At six o'clock sharp he let himself into her condo and was promptly confronted by Brutus and Catta. They seemed to be perturbed. "Everything okay with you guys?" he asked. "Did you pass your feline enteritis tests?" They seemed to be thinking, What is he doing here? . . . She's getting ready to go out. . . . She fed us early.

Polly heard him and appeared on the balcony, putting on her best gold earrings. "I'm on my way to a dinner meeting of the bird club. I told you about it, didn't I? I'm sure I did. But first I want you to read the letter on the foyer table."

The envelope was hotel stationery, postmarked Phoenix, Arizona. He read:

Dear Polly,

Forgive me for leaving in such a rude fashion. Henry seemed to think secrecy was advisable. We're being married tomorrow! You know how I have been feeling about living my own life. Well, Henry has convinced me that his Florence and my Harold (God rest their souls) would want us to look after each other in our remaining years. I don't know where we'll be living, so don't try to reach us here. And please don't mention that you've heard from us. I'll write again.

Fondly,
Maggie

P.S.
My ladies are being well taken care of.

"We'll talk about it when I get home," Polly said as she rushed off to the bird club.

Qwilleran huffed into his moustache. He believed not a word of Maggie's letter.

He shuffled home. What now? He was in the mood for a good dinner. He was still wearing his royal blue madras shirt.

As soon as he reached Unit Four, he phoned Jeffa Young.

"This is Qwill," he said in a businesslike way. "It occurred to me that there are things you should know about political correctness and self-preservation in a small town. Are you free for dinner? Do you know Tipsy's Tavern?"

"I've heard about the restaurant, and I'd love to meet her royal highness. I was just about to thaw some soup, but I'll put it back in the freezer. How nice of you to think of me."

Koko was sitting on the desk, eaves-dropping. "Well, I'm batting five hundred," Qwilleran told him with satisfaction.

It was a successful evening. She was delighted with the log cabin, the Tipsy myth, the honest food, and the grandmotherly service. He asked her about Baltimore and Coeur d'Alene, her grandchildren and her late husband's import business. He also gave her the Qwilleran Orientation Lecture, for which she was grateful.

"Do you have any questions?" he asked as the evening was coming to a close. The restaurant was emptying. They were lingering over coffee.

"Yes!" she said. "What is a pasty?" She pronounced it wrong, of course.

With her education completed, they drove back to Indian Village, and he dropped her at her doorstep. At his own condo Koko was waiting excitedly; there was a message on the machine. It was a responsibility Koko took seriously.

Polly's voice said, "Call me when you come home, Qwill. I have things to tell you."

He suspected she had startling information about the migration of certain spe-
cies of birds. He decided to wait until
morning.

twelve

Qwilleran phoned Polly Tuesday morning at about eight-thirty, when she was preparing to leave for the library. "Good morning! You called last night," he said with the genial voice of one who has slept well after a good dinner.

Her reply had the frantic tone of one who is a little late for work. "Where were you? I called three times before leaving a message."

"I took our new neighbor, Jeffa Young, to dinner at Tipsy's."

"Oh, really? How did that happen?"

"I ran into her earlier in the day, and she invited me in for a drink."

"Oh, really? Is she interesting?"

"Very. How was the bird club dinner? Did you have four-and-twenty blackbirds baked in a pie?"

She ignored the quip. "Last night I called to tell you what one of our members heard from a sheriff's deputy. The license plate on the killer's car was not only out-of-state but it was stolen!"

"It could have been stolen by a local boy. Or girl." Residents of Moose County liked to think that wrongdoers came from somewhere else.

"Well, you'll have to excuse me. I'm late. Would you be good enough to run over and feed the cats?"

"Yellow package or green package?"

"Yellow. Thanks. Talk to you later."

Qwilleran said, "I'll be right back" to Koko and Yum Yum and hurried to Unit One. He had done this service for Polly's cats many times before, but they always regarded him like a burglar, or a bill-collector at best.

"Are you two gourmands ready for a big bowl of health?" he asked jovially as he poured dry food from the yellow package. They looked at the bowl and looked questioningly at him, as if expecting the green package.

"That's what she ordered, and that's what you're getting," he said as he hurried out the front door.

He arrived home in time to grab the telephone and hear the cheerful voice of the young managing editor saying, "Hi, Qwill! Have you heard that there's an astrologer in town? You could get her to do your horoscope and then write a column about her."

Brusquely he replied, "Jill Handley could have her horoscope done and then write a column on it."

"I thought you were hard up for material."

"Not *that* hard up."

The snappish tone was nothing new; the two men enjoyed bickering.

Junior said, "This is Tuesday. May I ask when you expect to file your copy for today's paper?"

"Have I ever missed a deadline? . . . Is there any news in today's newspaper?"

"Amanda had a scrap with the mayor at the council meeting last night."

"That's not news. They've been scrapping for ten years."

"Homer Tibbitt is in the hospital getting his knees fixed."

"It's about time! His bones are very loosely connected."

"When you're his age, Qwill, you'll be loosely connected, too."

"I'll rust out long before I'm ninety-eight. . . . Any suspects in the shooting?"

"Nope."

"Any inside information on the Big One?"

"It must be on the way," Junior said. "Cats are getting nervous, and men over fifty are getting crotchety." There came a long, loud yowl from the foyer that could be heard in downtown Pickax. "I heard your master's voice, Qwill. Talk to you later."

Then came an unusual sound from the living room: *Shhh . . . shhh . . . sshhh . . .* followed by a *thud.*

Koko was crouched on the coffee table, looking over the edge. The three red apples, along with their over-turned wood bowl, were nestled in the deep pile of the Danish rug.

That's a new wrinkle, Qwilleran thought. . . . What's the reason? Where's the thrill? "No!" he said loudly. "That's forbidden fruit!"

Nonchalantly the cat jumped to the floor and walked casually to the utility room, where he could be heard scratching in his commode. Could he possibly associate the apples with the delivery man who had brought them? He had howled at the moment of the man's murder! Even for a cat with Koko's paranormal propensities, this was too much to expect. Perhaps he sensed that the apples were artificial, and that fact disturbed him. Perhaps he was simply curious. How would a smooth-as-porcelain wooden bowl slide across a smooth-as-glass wooden table? Or he might have been testing the rug; the *thud* was less satisfying than the *thunk* of a book on a carpeted floor—or the crash of a clay plant pot dropping thirteen feet.

Qwilleran reflected that the Siamese were living in fairly snug quarters, compared to their domain in the converted apple barn; Koko might be making a subtle suggestion. . . . Apple barn! Was something wrong at their summer address?

Taking his thousand words for the "Qwill Pen," he drove first to the hundred-year-old barn on the outskirts of Pickax. He inspected the premises, inside and out. Everything was in order, except for a small mouse, starved to death on the kitchen floor. Had that been Koko's chief concern?

I'm a fool, Qwilleran told himself. I'm trying to read messages where none exist! Koko pushed that bowl of apples off the table because he felt like pushing a bowl of apples off the table!

He handed in his copy on Misty Morghan's batiks in time to make the noon deadline. Passing the feature department he was beckoned by Mildred Riker. "Could you and Polly come over some night to see our new sofa and have a little supper?"

"How little?" he asked. "If it's too little, I'm not interested."

"You can have seconds—and thirds," she said. "This weekend I made my famous Old Shoe Soup, and we'll have it with crusty bread and a cheese board, then an avocado salad, then pumpkin pie."

"It all sounds good except the soup," he said.

"Did you never hear how I got the recipe?'' She asked the department secretary to take her calls for a few minutes, and then she told her story:

"When I was very small, I used to visit my grandparents' farm south of Trawnto. That was before Moose County had tractors. We were always thirty years behind the times. They had horse-drawn farm equipment and lots of hired hands who had to be fed an enormous dinner in the middle of the day. Once a week my grandmother would make bean soup in a big washtub. It was full of carrots, onions, potatoes, and celery, and it smelled so good when it was cooking. My grandmother said it was because she always put an old shoe in with the beans and stuff. She let me stand on a chair and see for myself as she stirred it with a long-handled wooden spoon. Sure enough! There it was! An old farm boot. I asked her if she had to have a different boot each week, and she said yes. All the farmers and farmhands in the community saved their old boots for Grandma's soup!

"When I went home, I told my mother, and I suffered the first disenchantment of my life. She said it was a large ham bone. I insisted I could see the shoestrings. She said there was a lot of meat left on the bone. Some kids were disenchanted when they learned the truth about Santa Claus, but I was disenchanted when I learned the truth about the old shoe. And I still think of my grandmother every time I make bean soup."

Qwilleran said, "I dare you to print the recipe on the food page."

"Someone would fail to get the joke," Mildred said, "and I'd be arrested by the Board of Health."

On the way to the municipal parking lot, Qwilleran met MacWhannell. "How'd you like the rally, Mac?"

"Good show! They collected over two thousand for the Ruff Abbey Fund. What did you think of Jeffa Young?"

"Fine woman. You're lucky to get her for your staff."

"I hear you took her to dinner. Is she going to do your chart?"

"The subject never came up, Mac."

"She's doing Gordie's and mine. You should have one, Qwill."

"I'll bear it in mind." This was Qwilleran's

way of turning down a suggestion. . . . but the suggestion would not go away. At home Polly called him, speaking in an apologetic way.

"Qwill, I've been asked to get some information from you—by hook or by crook."

"Asked by whom? It doesn't sound good."

"It's perfectly respectable. It's for a Christmas gift. All I need is the place and hour of your birth."

"Oh-oh! It sounds like one of Mildred's tricks. Tell her I don't want a horoscope. I'd rather have a handpainted necktie with a boa constrictor on it."

After hanging up, he huffed into his moustache. The subterfuge had gone too far. Susan would be blackmailing him—in a genteel way. The only solution was to go to Jeffa Young and make a clean breast of it—but not right now. Koko was on the desk, sniffing at the day's mail. He could tell which envelopes came from people having cats or dogs. . . . One was from Burgess Campbell, a printout of *Phineas Ford's Fabulous Collection*:

Back in the 1920s there was a feed-and-seed dealer in Brrr Township who was a real nice guy—hardworking, honest with his customers, and devoted to his wife. They had no children, and it was his way of showing kindness and understanding by taking her for a ride every Sunday afternoon in his Maxwell. Or was it a Model T? They would buy strawberries or a pumpkin, depending on the season, and stop at an ice cream parlor in town for a soda.

His wife also liked to visit antique shops. She never bought anything—just looked. Every town had an antique shop and every farmhouse had a barnful of junk and a sign that said ANTIQUES. As she wandered through the jumble of castoffs, her husband trudged behind her, looking left and right and wondering why people bought such stuff.

Once in a while he played a little joke on her as they drove. She would say, "Stop! There's an antique shop!" And he would say, "Where? Where?"

and speed up. Sometimes she'd insist that he turn around and go back.

On one of these occasions she had her own way, and they visited a farmhouse collection of this and that, Phineas traipsing dutifully behind his wife. Suddenly he saw something that aroused his curiosity, and he asked the farmwife what it was.

"A scamadiddle," she said. "Early American. Very rare. Found only in the Midwest."

"How much do you want for it?"

"Oh, a dollar, I guess," she said.

"Give you ninety cents." Phineas was no fool.

He carried it to the car and put it on the backseat, causing his wife to ask, "What's that thing?"

"What thing?"

"That thing on the backseat."

"That's a scamadiddle," he said casually, as if he bought one every day. "Early American, you know. Very rare. Found only in the Midwest."

"Oh," she said. "What are you going to do with it?"

"Put it in the china cabinet."

Every weekend after that, Phineas found pleasure in antiquing, forever searching for another scamadiddle. One Sunday he found it! Now he had two! He was a collector!

They began to travel farther afield, into adjoining counties, and to Phineas's delight there was an occasional scamadiddle to be found. The shopkeepers, knowing his interest, kept their eyes open and produced an occasional treasure. He was paying two dollars now—and no dickering. He built a room onto their house, lined with shelves and one glass case for choice examples.

The breakthrough came when another collector died, and Phineas bought his entire collection. A magazine called him the Scamadiddle King. He built another, larger room and paid the high dollar for the few remaining scamadiddles. Three museums were bidding to buy the Phineas Ford Collection posthumously.

Then tragedy struck! One fateful night his house was struck by lightning and burned to the ground, reducing the entire scamadiddle collection to ashes.

And that's why—today—there's not a single scamadiddle to be found in the United States.

Qwilleran chuckled long and lustily before phoning the antique shop. "Susan," he said seriously, "do you ever run across any scamadiddles in your travels?"

"Any what?"

He repeated it and spelled it.

"I see whirligigs and niddy-noddies, but I've never seen a scamadiddle—but then folk things aren't my specialty. Iris Cobb would know, if she were here."

"Well, when you go to that big show in New York, will you inquire around?"

"How high are you willing to go?" she asked.

"Not over a thousand."

thirteen

On Wednesday Qwilleran went downtown to pick up Polly's groceries. In front of the Pickax People's National Bank of America he came upon Burgess Campbell and friend, and he said heartily, "Professor Moriarty, I believe! Are you planning to rob the bank?"

There was a momentary handclasp. "Sherlock! How strange you should ask! Alexander has been sniffing out the security traps."

"Shouldn't you be in the lecture hall, Professor?"

"Not until one o'clock. Would you like to audit Political Foibles of the Early Nineteenth Century? I have a new boffo about Congress that you probably never heard."

Opening each lecture with a joke, he maintained, put his students in a relaxed and receptive mode, and no one was ever late.

Qwilleran declined the invitation. "Only if you know the one about the preacher who thought his bicycle had been stolen. . . . But let me tell you that your scamadiddle scam is a gem! Of all the tales I've collected, it's the only real leg-puller."

"I hope you can credit my father. Prentis Campbell III. He was an unreconstructed joker."

From there Qwilleran went to the library to break the news that he would not be joining Polly for leftovers that evening.

He stopped at the circulation desk to stroke Mac, one of the resident cats, and inquired about Katie.

"She had to go to the vet to have her teeth cleaned." The clerk looked up at the glass-enclosed office on the mezzanine. "Mrs. Duncan has somebody with her."

"No hurry. I'll browse." Browsing among the catalogued, jacketed, well-bound, dust-free titles in the public library lacked the sense of adventure he had known at Edd's Editions. A part of his life had gone up in smoke.

After a while a man walked down the stairs, and Qwilleran walked up.

"That was Dr. Emerson from Black Creek," Polly said. "He wants to donate a suitable memorial to his late mother. She was an eminent churchwoman, an enthusiastic reader, and a lifelong knitter. . . . Excuse me if I start my lunch. . . ." From her lunchbox arose the familiar whiff of tuna.

He said, "I'll pick up your groceries, but I'm afraid I can't have dinner tonight."

"Oh, really?"

He paused long enough for her to imagine the worst scenario, then said, "It's Wetherby Goode's night off, and he's taking me to the curling club. I'm treating to dinner."

"Where will you go?"

"To the Nutcracker Inn—just to check it out. If the food and atmosphere are good, you and I will go—preferably before snow flies."

He left her before she could offer him a carrot stick and drove to the art center.

The parking lot was filled to overflowing, and the manager, Barb Ogilvie, greeted him with excitement. "Qwill! Look at the response to your column about batik-printing! Standing room only! Do you want to squeeze in? It's almost over."

He chose to wait in the downstairs gallery until the scraping of chairs, hubbub of voices, and chugging of departing vehicles told him the program was over. Misty was thrilled with the attendance and the number who signed up for the course: eight women and one man, some of them from Lockmaster County. "This is my week!" she said to Qwilleran. "First the really super column that you wrote—then the great turnout—and then, this afternoon, I sign the contract for ten shafthouse batiks. My patron doesn't want the commission or his identity to be known until the project is finished, but I'll give you a sneak peek at the sketches if you'll promise not to tell."

The ten shafthouses were basically similar, but the artist's eye had discerned their individuality. The structures were sketched from different angles, and wildlife was introduced: a doe with fawn, a raccoon, crows chasing a hawk, an antlered buck, a pair of squirrels.

Misty said, "I normally ask two thousand for a three-by-four, custom-designed, but I'll have to buy extra vats and hire students to help, and Theo thinks I should ask five thousand. But that sounds rather high to me."

Qwilleran agreed with her husband. "Your patron sounds less like an art lover and more like an investor who thinks shafthouses will disappear from the landscape and the batiks will appreciate in value."

On the way out he had a few words with the manager. Barb Ogilvie loved her new job, was teaching a class in art-knitting, and had started dating Misty's brother-in-law.

Walking to the parking lot, Qwilleran said, "Hi!" to a tall man who was taking long strides toward the building. The tall man made an equally expressionless response. Wait a minute! Qwilleran told himself; that was Don Exbridge! He's going in to sign the contract for ten batiks! He has no interest in art and had no interest in shafthouses until his recent letter to the editor—and that was of questionable sincerity.

Hurrying to the cell phone in his van, Qwilleran called the building he had just left and asked to speak with Misty.

Barb said, "She's just gone into an important conference—"

"This is more important—and confidential, Barb. Qwill speaking. Have her take the call in your office. Don't mention my name."

Misty came to the phone with wariness in her hello.

"This is Qwill," he said. "I saw your patron entering the building and know who he is—a shrewd operator. Take Theo's advice. Ask five thousand. He can afford it, and the art is worth it. Also, ask innocently what he intends to do with them. His reaction should be revealing. If he gives you an answer, it should be interesting, though not necessarily honest."

* * *

"You drive!" the weatherman said to Qwilleran when they met at six P.M. "I've got the jitters." As they headed for the Nutcracker Inn, he explained. "I just got a bummer of a letter from my ex-wife—first one since the divorce five years ago. She wants us to get together again! How do I handle it? Ignore it? Tell her to drop dead? There's no point in trying to explain reasonably; she's like a bulldog—won't let go. I like my lifestyle, my job, my friends, the idea of having relatives in Horseradish. Also, there's a girl down there that I like a lot—nothing serious."

Qwilleran said, "I suspected you didn't go down there to visit your sisters and your cousins and your aunts. Why did your marriage break up, if I may ask?"

"She wanted me to go back to school, get another degree, and become a serious scientist. Let's face it, I'm an entertainer, and weather is my gimmick! But she nagged and nagged and nagged. Why did your marriage break up, Qwill?"

"In-law trouble. She married me without her parents' permission. In the first place they scorned the media, and I was a gypsy-journalist, working for a different paper every two years, taking assignments all over the globe. They talked her into divorcing me, saying I wasn't good enough for her—I'd never amount to anything—I drank. Soon after, she had a nervous breakdown, for which I was blamed, of course. Her parents were loaded, but they sent me her hospital bills. After that I really hit the bottle. Couldn't hold a job. Almost killed myself before I came to my senses and got help. . . . I usually don't go into these details."

"How would you feel, Qwill, if she suddenly suggested a reconciliation?"

"She died a few years ago—in an institution."

For a while there was nothing to say, until Qwilleran remarked, "With so many failed marriages, one forgets how many are successful: the Lanspeaks, the MacWhannells, Junior and Jody Goodwinter, Fran Brodie's parents, the MacGillivrays, Lori and Nick Bamba, the Buster Ogilvies, Homer Tibbitt and Rhoda—"

"The Tibbitts are practically newlyweds," Wetherby said.

"At their age, every year counts ten. . . . What about the mayor? I never hear anything about his home life."

"He has a wife, no kids. Betty's a homebody; hizzoner goes out selling stocks and bonds, playing golf, and pressing the flesh. His wife runs a mail-order business for her handcrafts. Have you heard of Betty Blythe's Bunwarmers?"

"No! And I'm gripping the steering wheel to avoid falling off the seat. What are they?"

"Handmade baskets with handwoven napkins for keeping dinner rolls warm. She advertises in craft magazines and does very well."

Only one old building remained in Black Creek, which had been a thriving town on a busy waterway in the nineteenth century. The Limburger mansion had been purchased by the Klingenschoen Foundation and was now making its debut as a country inn. There had been magnificent black walnut trees in the vicinity, and the mansion had the treasured black walnut woodwork. Hence the name: the Nutcracker Inn.

Qwilleran said to Wetherby, "I was in this house when the old man was alive—an eccentric old geezer. There was a cuckoo clock in the front hall. It's gone."

"A good thing, too!" was the reply. "It would have driven the guests crazy. Or perhaps I should say: cuckoo."

When the innkeeper welcomed them, Qwilleran asked about facilities for lodging and was told there were four large rooms on the second floor, two suites on the third floor, and five semi-housekeeping cabins down by the creek.

"Open all year round?"

"That depends what happens after snow flies. The K Foundation will make the decision. I'm Chicago-based, under contract to train staff and get the place running, then hire permanent innkeepers from the locality."

"I know the ideal couple," Qwilleran said. "Lori and Nick Bamba have the personality for innkeeping and a certain amount of experience."

"Good! Tell them to apply to the K Foundation."

When they were seated in the dining room, Wetherby said, "I remember the

Bambas. They had a B&B at Breakfast Island. What happened?"

"The weather didn't cooperate. Lori is working at the Pet Plaza now."

"Kennebeck is having its annual roundup of stray cats before the Big One moves in. Any stray that's adopted will be spayed or neutered—with Tipsy's Tavern paying for it."

"Tipsy herself was a stray, seventy years ago," Qwilleran said.

"Did you see that teaser ad for a new recreation center in Pickax? What do you suppose it is?"

"Who knows? They promise fun for the whole family."

"And did you see the letters to the editor in Monday's paper? They're all nuts! Did you hear that we have a professional astrologer living in the Village? I'm thinking of having my horoscope done. She does it in depth. Why don't you have yours done, Qwill? I'm a Scorpio, sexy and talkative. What are you?"

"A Gemini—talented, likable, sensitive, kind, generous—"

"Sure," Wetherby said.

"How about filling me in on curling—before we go to the club? How many on a team?"

"Four and a captain, called a skip."

"How big is the rink?"

"A little wider than a bowling alley—and longer. The target, called the 'house,' is a circle of concentric rings, and the bull's-eye is called the 'tee.' "

"And what are the stones and brooms called?"

"Stones and brooms."

"What does the skip do?"

"He reads the ice. There's fast ice and slow ice. He calls the plays: when to sweep, when to take out an opponent's stone, how much weight to put into the throw. A lot of strategy and a lot of skill go into the game. Also a lot of suspense for the watchers. It won't be crowded tonight, but you should see it when they have a tournament—called a bonspiel."

The Pickax Curling Club had been built out in the country where land was affordable, and there was plenty of space for parking during a bonspiel. It looked, everyone said, like a Swiss chalet, and the interior expressed friendliness, the essence of the sport of curling.

Qwilleran later described his reactions in his personal journal:

Joe and I started in the warming room, where I saw a few persons I knew: Theo and Misty Morghan . . . Fran Brodie and Dr. Prelligate . . . Hixie Rice and Dwight Somers . . . Jeffa Young with (of all people!) Kirt Nightingale. Was he trying to sell her some books? Or was she lining him up for a natal chart? Dwight thanked me for recommending him to Cass Young and said he could do the builder a lot of good.

While chatting with the Morghans, I heard something enlightening. Misty's secret patron (I happen to know he's Don Exbridge) dropped in at her studio to inquire if she could meet a certain deadline. He said they're for use in a large restaurant with balconies, and the batiks would hang from the balcony railings. The restaurant wanted to open before snow flies. It would help if she could deliver a few of the batiks, if not the whole order.

So that explained why Ernie Kemple's offer for the building was rejected! Exbridge is going into business with the former owner of Otto's Tasty Eats!

Joe pointed out Cass Young—a good-looking man, tall and straight like his mother. Cass and the members of the ice committee were dealing with a problem, so we didn't intrude. It appeared that the new compressor machine was not maintaining the ice properly, and there was a bonspiel scheduled for Saturday. The technician had to come from Bixby, and he had a prior emergency, but he would come late if someone would promise to let him in.

Mechanical equipment, restrooms and lockers were on a lower level, but we could see a small trophy area at the foot of the stairs. There was a commemorative curling stone on a pedestal and a pair of crossed pickaxes on the wall—the same insigne that appears in the small pin worn by members.

In the warming room a chalkboard listed the evening's matches. Through a plate-glass window the rinks could be seen. Someone was planing the ice, which would then be sprayed with water to provide a pebbled effect; if the ice was too slick, the stones would fly off into the next county. During the game, players would sweep the ice with brooms to get the "ice dust" and water out of the path of the moving stones.

When the matches began and we went to the spectators' gallery, I discovered what a civilized sport this was! No fights on the ice . . . no abusive shouts from the onlookers!

"Who casts the first stone?" I asked Joe.

The first player approached the hack—the footboard that keeps a curler from flying down the ice with the stone. There was a moment of concentration—then a crouch and a lunge, and the stone went gliding serenely down the rink. To me that dynamic lunge created a moment of suspense like the baseball pitcher's windup, the discus-thrower's spin, or the caber-tosser's stagger with towering pole.

I found the whole experience hypnotic: watching the stone as it journeyed across the ice, curling around an obstacle, traveling not too far but far enough. How do they do it? With a twist of the wrist? Or with sheer will power? Meanwhile cries from players and spectators fill the arena. "Sweep! . . . Take it out! Good rock! Lay it up! . . . Off the broom! . . . We got the hammer! . . . Good weight!"

Later, in the warming room, I met Cass Young and said I'd like to join the club. He signaled to a young red-haired woman. "New member! Grab him before he gets away!"

She brought an application card and asked if I'd like to sign up for instruction.

Then a wild-eyed member of the ice committee rushed up and said, "I can't wait for the technician! Gotta take my wife to the hospital! She's due!"

"I'll stay," said Cass. "Go home! Don't worry. . . . I hope it's a boy!" he called after the disappearing figure.

"I hope it's a girl!" said the redhead.

On the way home Wetherby said, "Do you know who the redhead is? Don Exbridge's second wife. She's in the process of divorcing him."

"I heard about that," Qwilleran said, "but when I met her last year at a dinner party, she seemed like a mousy little creature."

"Don likes mousy," Wetherby said. "He wants to be the whole cheese. Actually, Robyn—that's spelled with a Y—has a good personality. The red hair is something new."

Qwilleran said, "When Susan divorced Don, she started calling everyone 'darling' and opened a posh antique shop. What do you suppose Robyn will do with her divorce settlement?"

"She's already resumed her former occupation: free-lance manicurist. House calls only . . . Do you think you'll take curling instruction?"

"I think not. I'm a professional spectator, and my hobby is people-watching. . . . Would you come in for a nightcap? I have some especially good Scotch."

"That seems like an appropriate cap on the evening."

When they reached The Willows and let themselves into Unit Four, a horrendous sound met their ears.

"My God! What's that?" Wetherby gasped.

A gut-wrenching growl ended in an ear-splitting shriek.

Qwilleran groaned, dreading the message and fearing another volunteer had been struck down. "It's Koko," he said hoarsely.

"I heard it the other night, through the wall, and thought the wolves were back in Moose County. . . . Is it something he ate?"

"It's a mystery." Qwilleran chose not to reveal the family secret. "Let's have that nightcap."

After Wetherby had his nip of Scotch and returned to Unit Three to take a shower—

audible through the thin walls—Qwilleran phoned the night desk at the *Something.* . . . No, they said, there had been no incident on the police beat.

fourteen

Qwilleran was roused early by a phone call from his next-door neighbor. "Bad news, Qwill! A guy at the station who belongs to the curling club and knows I do—he just phoned to say that Cass Young fell down those stone steps to the lower level and killed himself! May have hit his head on that curling stone on display . . . He was waiting for the technician, you remember. Could have been passing the time with a beer. Could have been in too much of a hurry to get to the restroom . . . Are you there? Are you awake?"

"I'm listening," Qwilleran said. "I don't know what to say."

"It'll be on the next hourly news. Just thought I'd alert you. . . . Had a good time last night."

"So did I."

It was too late to go back to bed and too early to get up, and as Qwilleran pushed the button on the coffeemaker, he thought, forget the beer. . . . Forget the restroom. His moustache was twitching, and he tamped it with his knuckles. Koko knew something murderous had happened, and Koko was never wrong. The public would prefer to think it an accident: Crime was something they wanted to think "did not happen here." How soon they forgot the unsavory incidents of the past!

Within minutes the phone rang again. It was Susan, speaking without her usual flippancy. "Qwill! We've had a tragedy on River Road! Early this morning I was awakened by vehicle lights and voices outside my window. The sheriff's car was next door. I went out in my robe, thinking something dreadful had happened to Jeffa, but they were notifying her that her son had suffered a fatal accident at the curling club! I phoned Dr. Diane, and she came rushing over, and Jeffa asked me to call her daughter in Idaho. . . . Isn't it awful, Qwill?"

"Is there anything at all that I could do?"

"Well, Jeffa had me call Mac MacWhannell, and he's going to take charge of everything, but you could pick up the daughter at the airport. She'll arrive on the five-thirty shuttle. Her name is Angela Parsons."

"Jeffa strikes me as a strong woman," Qwilleran said.

"Yes, she's not one to collapse, but Diane gave her a light sedative, and she's sleeping. A caregiver will stay with her till Angela arrives. . . . Isn't it terrible? She lost her husband this year—and now this!"

Qwilleran suppressed the urge to go downtown for breakfast and eavesdrop on the gossip about Cass Young's faults as a builder and his friendship with the second Mrs. Exbridge. He chose to work on his Friday column, announcing the winners of the haiku contest. Yum Yum, always filled with contentment when he was reading or writing, dozed on the blue cushion atop the refrigerator. Koko was restless, pushing things off tables. Pencils, books, and the bowl of wooden apples landed on the floor.

At two o'clock Qwilleran picked up his newspaper at the gatehouse and found full details of the "accident" with statements from the technician (who had found the body and reported it) and the medical examiner and the officers of the club. The last person to see him alive was quoted. A sidebar described the clubhouse, and an engineer explained the equipment necessary to maintain the quality of ice. The sports page went into the history of curling.

"Everything," Qwilleran muttered, "except the salient question: Who pushed him?"

Working on Friday's "Qwill Pen" column was a welcome respite after the disturbing implications of Koko's midnight message. Most contest entrants squeezed a personal note as well as a short poem on a postal card. Eight winners had been chosen by the three judges: Polly Duncan, Junior Goodwinter, and Rhoda Tibbitt.

A fifth-grader wrote: "If I win, I'll give my yellow pencil to my two cats, Nippy and Tucky."

Catnap
Fur pillow on my chair—
*   three ears, two tails.*
one nose, no paws.

The entries ranged from whimsical to thought-provoking. A retired nurse explained, "I worked for a large industrial firm Down Below, and one of the bookkeepers died after being on the payroll for thirty years. Her obituary in the employee newspaper consisted of only eleven words. It made me cry."

Obituary
She had such pretty white hair
*   and was always*
very pleasant.

Birds and butterflies were favorite topics, and a birdwatcher won a yellow pencil for this one.

Birdling
A baby phoebe,
*   drunk with youth,*
is staggering on the breeze.

Another nature-lover wrote, "This actually happened to me twenty years ago, and I've never forgotten it."

Monarch
Once a pair of orange wings
alighted on my finger,
and I smiled for days!

A student in her senior year in high school submitted this moody reverie:

Listen
The wet sounds of a rainy day . . .
Why do they make me feel
so wistful?

A man wrote, "I'm the dad of a two-year-old and a four-year-old who are both bursting with energy. Can I submit two poems?"

Rocking Horse
Hurry, child!
Ask your questions.
Tomorrow there may be no answers.

Tricycle
Hurry, child!

Find your answers.
Tomorrow there may be no questions.

Only one entry was submitted anonymously.

Lost Love
Too warm . . . too kind . . .
*   too good . . . too near . . .*
too much!

When Qwilleran handed in his copy to Junior, the managing editor—who was a father of two—said that his favorite verses were submitted by the father of two.

"That figures," Qwilleran said. "My favorite was a nonwinner. Apparently a fifth-grade teacher in Sawdust City assigned her class to enter the contest—or else. One rebellious youth submitted: 'My teacher wears thick glasses . . . and makes us do things . . . we don't want to do.' I think I'll send him a yellow pencil for honesty and bravery."

"What's your topic for next Tuesday?"

"I haven't decided. That's four days away. The way things are going in this town, someone might bomb the *Moose County Something.*"

Before leaving the building, he went into the Ready Room and found Roger MacGillivray sitting with his feet on the table, waiting for another assignment—and probably hoping he could get home to dinner. It had been his byline on the banner story.

"Compliments on your Cass Young coverage. It was very thorough."

"My coverage is always thorough," Roger said. "It's the editors who cut it down."

"Is there a story behind the story?"

"Only that Cass had a slider on his left foot that should have been covered with a gripper—a rash oversight for someone known for preaching safety."

Qwilleran smoothed his moustache. "Unless someone removed the gripper after the so-called accident."

"Hey! That's an interesting angle! Stick around for a while. There's some coffee left," Roger said with sudden animation.

"I can't. I'm picking up his sister at the airport."

* * *

When the shuttle flight arrived from Minneapolis, Qwilleran scanned the passengers in search of a tall, straight, dark-haired counterpart of Jeffa Young. No one fitted the description. There were business daytrippers with briefcases or laptops, hikers with backpacks, shoppers with tote bags from the best stores. One woman disembarked slowly, casting disapproving glances left and right.

"Mrs. Parsons?" he guessed.

She nodded.

"I'm to drive you to your mother's house. I'm Jim Qwilleran, a neighbor of hers. Do you have luggage?"

"A black zipper overnight."

She was shorter than her mother and of less striking appearance. "How far is it?" she asked, as if it mattered.

"About a fifteen-minute ride. You're not seeing us at our best, because you're too late for the autumn color and too early for the winter wonderland. We're expecting the storm called the Big One any day now. How long do you plan to stay?"

"Just long enough to convince her to move to Idaho. She should have come to us in the first place. We can offer a more congenial environment, you know—a family situation with grandchildren, birthday cakes, Thanksgiving dinners, and all that."

Qwilleran huffed into his moustache. "In the short time Mrs. Young has been here she seems to have enjoyed making friends, pursuing her hobby, and finding an outlet for her professional skills."

"She can do all that in Idaho."

He cleared his throat. "I met your brother for the first time at the curling club last night and was shocked to hear about his accident. You have my deepest sympathy."

"What do they say caused the accident?" she asked coolly.

"A fall down a flight of stone stairs after everyone else had left. He had graciously offered to wait for a technician who was traveling a long distance to make emergency repairs. The man found Cass at the foot of the stairs."

"Did they say whether he'd been drinking?" she asked sharply.

"It wasn't a consideration, apparently. . . . How many grandchildren does Jeffa have, Mrs. Parsons?"

"We have two girls and a boy, between four and eight. They're all excited about meeting their grandmother for the first time."

"What attracted you to Idaho? I presume you're a native of Maryland."

"I'm interested in the preservation of the environment, and I went vacationing in the northwest part of the state and fell in love with it! You should visit the area. If you like it around here, you'll like Idaho ten times more."

"Thank you for the suggestion. It's something to keep in mind."

When they arrived in Jeffa's driveway, he told her to go in and he would bring the luggage. Mother and daughter were embracing in the doorway when he pulled away.

"I didn't see any tears," Qwilleran told Polly when he reported to her condo later in the evening. She had invited him to a soup supper and had prepared his favorite baked potato soup—a cream base flavored with cheese and bacon bits and loaded with chunks of yesterday's baked potatoes, skins and all. It was another of Polly's leftover masterpieces.

"What was the daughter like?" she asked.

"Not as handsome or sophisticated as Jeffa. She doesn't expect to stay long, judging by the size of her overnight bag. She didn't show any signs of mourning for her brother. I wonder what the funeral arrangements will be."

"My spies at the library know all the particulars," Polly said. "Mac MacWhannell is taking care of everything according to Jeffa's wishes: cremation, no funeral, but a memorial service to be planned by the two curling clubs. . . . I hope Jeffa stays here. Big Mac is depending on her help with the tax rush. He was being very solicitous at Amanda's rally. One can't help wondering. . . . You know, his wife is terminally ill."

Qwilleran said, "I'll be willing to bet that Jeffa stays here."

fifteen

When Qwilleran was preparing the cats' breakfast, they sat watching him intently, Koko looking intelligent and Yum Yum looking hungry. Speak to them on your own intellectual level, he believed, and they will respond accordingly. He said to Koko, "Will you reiterate your recent midnight message? If you still suspect foul play, slap the floor three times with your tail."

Koko's tail remained virtually glued to the vinyl, but the doorbell rang, and Susan Exbridge was on the doorstep. "Darling, I'm on my way to the shop, but I have news."

"Come in!" he said. "Have a cup of coffee."

"Your coffee is wonderful, but don't let me stay. I'm meeting a fabulously affluent customer." She went directly to the loungy sofa. "Love this rug! It's not my taste, but it's so sensually correct with your furniture."

He served coffee. She recognized his Jensen tray. He admired her earrings. She said they were hallmarked English silver buttons. He said, "Excuse me while I finish feeding the cats." They were on the kitchen counter and had finished feeding themselves.

Finally he joined his guest with a coffee mug and said, "Well, I delivered Angela to her mother's house, as requested."

"What did you think of her?"

"To tell the truth, she seemed cold and calculating and not at all concerned about her brother's death. She doesn't have her mother's commanding stature, I noticed."

"She's a stepdaughter," Susan told him. "When Jeffa married Mr. Young, he was a widower with a daughter. Then they had a son together."

Qwilleran nodded. "Understandable. And what's your news?"

"Darling, I don't need to tell you how thin the walls are in this development! Last night I heard an awful row next door between the two women. It was embarrassing!"

"But not so embarrassing that you didn't listen, I hope."

"Actually, I couldn't catch a word, but I heard a door slam, and then all was quiet. . . . But this morning the airport limousine came for Angela! She's gone! I think Jeffa is staying here! Big Mac will have his help during the tax rush, and I may get my hands on that Hepplewhite sideboard for the New York show!"

"Hmff!" was Qwilleran's only comment.

"Mac has come to the rescue like a big brother, making all arrangements. He's treasurer of the curling club, you know, so he has a double interest in the case."

"Have you talked to Robyn?"

"Yes, and I feel so sorry for her. She and Jeffa are the chief mourners, and it's very touching how they're consoling each other. Donald is probably laughing his head off, rat that he is!"

"Yow!" came a loud comment from Koko, who was on the table in the foyer, as if to speed the parting guest.

"Well, I must tear myself away," Susan said. "Thanks for the coffee, and don't forget: I'm interested in the St. Louis pitcher!"

After she had left, Koko continued to sit on the carved oak glove box, one of his favorite perches in recent days. He treated it like a pedestal for the sculptural poses he liked to strike.

"Vanity! Vanity!" Qwilleran observed.

He turned his attention to the speech he was scheduled to make that evening. At the urging of his friend, Kip McDiarmid, editor of the *Lockmaster Ledger,* he had consented to be after-dinner speaker at a meeting of the literary club. His decision was influenced, no doubt, by the choice of meeting place, an upscale restaurant in horse country: the Palomino Paddock.

A veteran at making such speeches, he knew what his audience would want to know:

1. How he had learned his craft. (He gave credit to a tenth-grade English teacher, Mrs. Fisheye.)
2. His favorite authors. (Trollope, Flaubert, Nabokov and Mark Twain.)
3. What it's like to be a twice-weekly columnist. (Rough. Fun. Challenging. Underpaid.)
4. Where he gets his ideas. (I stare at my cat and he stares at me, eyeball to eyeball, and my brain goes into high gear.)
5. What he enjoyed most about writing for metropolitan newspapers Down Below. (The Press Clubs.)

Half serious and half entertaining, his talks always attracted a few more subscribers for the *Moose County Something.*

The dinner meeting at the Palomino Paddock was held in a private room— really two rooms thrown together because of the number of reservations. After the medallions of beef and the strawberries with peppercorn sauce, the *Lockmaster* editor introduced "the notorious columnist from the barbaric county to the north."

Qwilleran began by saying, "Needless to mention, I took the precaution of being vaccinated before venturing on this foreign soil."

The question-and-answer session that followed the talk included a discussion of haiku, since most of the audience had read that day's "Qwill Pen." Then Kip McDiarmid closed the program with a tongue-in-cheek haiku:

"Sick cat . . . Burnt toast . . . flat tire . . . computer down . . . business as usual."

It was after midnight when Qwilleran reached Indian Village. As he turned into River Road, a vehicle ahead of him pulled up to Amanda Goodwinter's condo. A passenger hurried indoors while Amanda herself brought luggage from the trunk.

Qwilleran was positive the guest was Maggie Sprenkle. Unfortunately it was too late to call Polly and ask if she knew what was happening.

Several questions bothered him: What is Maggie doing here? And why the apparent secrecy? Did she come by chartered plane? It was too late for scheduled flights.

Still without answers on Saturday morning, he chose to do some private sleuthing before involving Polly in the mystery. He went downtown for coffee and scones at the Scottish Bakery and found Burgess Campbell doing the same.

After the usual Celtic banter Qwilleran said, as a teaser, "I hear that Henry Zoller and Maggie Sprenkle have gone out west together and plan to marry."

"It'll never happen," the other man said. "She's a fanatic about cats, and he has an overfastidious objection to living under the same roof with an animal. Did you ever meet her late husband, Qwill? He was an easygoing fellow, famous for his rose garden. He used to invite me over to smell the roses, and he'd describe every bush as if it were a friend. All Henry's friends are on the golf course. . . . No, whoever spread the rumor about him and Maggie doesn't know what he's talking about."

"Someday," Qwilleran said, "I'd like to write a piece about the intelligent, well-mannered, unflappable Alexander. He's such a well-known dog-about-town!"

"That could be arranged," Burgess said, "although you shouldn't flatter him too much. I wouldn't want him getting a swelled head."

Qwilleran's next stop was the design studio. Amanda was in-house, scowling at the Saturday shoppers who were "just looking." Qwilleran hastened their departure by following them around like a store detective. It worked.

"How's the campaign going, Amanda?" he asked. "If you win, I want to be appointed ambassador to Lockmaster."

"I've got you slated for Secretary of Trash Collection," she snapped.

"I see you have a houseguest from out of town."

"What do you mean?"

"Didn't I see Maggie Sprenkle arriving last night?"

Amanda paused for only two heartbeats. "You didn't see her. Understand? You—did—not—see—her!"

"If you say so," he said, pleased at the hint of intrigue. "The person I didn't see must have arrived by chartered plane—in order to land under cover of darkness."

"No comment!" Her tight-lipped, down-turned mouth put an end to the conversation. But as he bowed out, she called after him, "Don't mention this to Polly!"

He drove home in a good mood. He now had a riddle to solve—something to stretch his wits. The sight of Koko waiting at the door suggested a solution.

"Want to go for a walk, old boy?" Qwilleran jingled the cat's harness and leash.

"Yow!" was the enthusiastic response. Whenever they walked outdoors, he rode on the man's shoulder; it gave him an elevated view and kept his paws clean. A firm hand on the leash prevented any impulsive moves.

They made their exit through the sliding glass doors in the living room, across the open deck, and down the steps to the riverbank trail. Well carpeted with fallen leaves, it rustled crisply underfoot.

Qwilleran headed north toward the other condo clusters, occasionally stopping to pick up a stone and hurl it across the river, or what was left of the rushing water. Drought had reduced it to a brook, conscientiously gurgling its way to the lake.

The scene had a Saturday quiet. The career folk who lived there were at work or shopping or catching up on domestic demands. Polly, for example, was organizing for winter, laundering and storing her warm-weather clothing, and bringing her winter wardrobe out of storage. It was a semi-annual ritual that Qwilleran had learned to respect.

When he reached the rear of The Birches, he knew that the first unit was Amanda's. He stopped to pitch a stone, hoping that Maggie would be in the living room, looking out the wall of glass. He had a good throwing arm, left over from his college days when he had been noticed by a scout for the Chicago Cubs. He flung several stones. Koko watched with interest. Once he yowled.

"Attaboy," Qwilleran said as he pitched another chunk of rock.

Koko yowled again.

Almost immediately there was tapping on the window and the sound of a sliding glass door.

Qwilleran looked up, feigning surprise, and saw an arm beckoning. Slowly he walked toward the deck and climbed the steps.

Maggie was in the doorway, putting a

finger to her lips, cautioning him to be silent.

Once inside the house, with the sliding door closed, he said in a hushed voice, "Maggie! What are you doing here? Why didn't you let us know?"

"It's a long story," she said wearily, "and I'm really not . . . at liberty . . . to discuss it."

This was hardly the effusive, grandiose Maggie everyone knew. Noticeably absent was the hugging.

Koko, perched on Qwilleran's shoulder, looked down at her and gurgled a throaty purr.

"He knows I'm a cat person," she said. "Sit down, Qwill. May I hold him?"

The leash was unsnapped, and Koko settled down on her lap. Though not a lapcat by temperament, he seemed to know that therapy was needed. She stroked him, and he purred lustily. "I've missed my ladies so much," she murmured.

"They're well and happy at the Pet Plaza," Qwilleran assured her. "I happened to be over there and noticed their names on the nameplates. . . . Is Henry with you, Maggie?"

Her answer was hesitant. "No, he didn't come—this time."

"Are felicitations in order?" he asked cheerfully. "Have the wedding bells been ringing?"

"No, I'm afraid they're postponed." She stroked the cat's fur nervously.

"You missed Amanda's rally. It was very well done. Derek sang an original campaign song. People said the event had every-thing—except Maggie Sprenkle." He knew that would touch a heartstring.

"Oh, Qwill!" she said pathetically. "I'm so upset. I'm not supposed to talk to any-one—until I've seen Henry's lawyer."

"I see . . . Well, I won't pry into your business, but if there's anything I can do—drive you anywhere or offer any brotherly advice—you know I'm trustworthy and sympathetic."

"I know."

"I heard someone speaking very highly of your late husband this morning."

"Jeremy . . . yes. We spent forty happy years together. . . . Qwill! I never intended to marry Henry! It was just . . . He had to leave town. He thought it would save face. . . . You won't breathe a word of this, will you?"

"Of course not, Maggie. I hope Henry isn't in any serious trouble."

"Did you know Cass Young?"

"Only by reputation until Wednesday night at the curling club, just a few hours before his accident."

"Henry thinks it wasn't an accident," Maggie said in a hushed voice.

"Yow!" said the cat on her lap.

"Oh, my! What a loud voice you have, Koko! Does he want to go home?"

"He's trying to tell you someone's coming. We'll leave." He grabbed Koko and headed for the sliding door. The doorbell rang.

"It'll be Mr. Bennett," Maggie said. "I'll stall until you get away."

Koko's body vibrated all the way home, supercharged by the intense stroking. Qwilleran kept a tight lead on the cat lest he should feel an impulse to take wing. It had been an exhilarating adventure for both of them. The man's strategy had worked: The cat seemed to have done all the right things on cue.

It had been revealed that Henry "had to

leave town." It sounded as if he were involved in financial dealings that were illegal, and now his attorney was trying to make a deal with the prosecutor, with Maggie as go-between. If so, it was serious business. Bennett was senior partner of Hasselrich Bennett & Barter. Despite the death of Hasselrich, the name of the firm had been retained, at least temporarily.

Qwilleran thought, Poor Maggie!—so outgoing, honest, and generous—still married to the memory of Jeremy and his rose garden, and lonesome for her five "ladies." And she was cast in an unfamiliar role of secrecy and complicity, with unknown stakes. . . . How would she explain the cat hairs on her clothing?

Back home and released from his harness, Koko sniffed noses with Yum Yum, who had come to meet him, and had a few laps of water and prowled around the house to see if anything new had been added. . . . after which he soared to the mantel and stayed there for the next two hours, stretched full length, exhausted by his adventure.

sixteen

Now Qwilleran had two hot news items he could not reveal—even to close friends: Henry's reason for leaving town and Maggie's secret return. The arrival of Jeffa's stepdaughter and her sudden angry departure were already stale news on the Pickax grapevine.

This was the evening for viewing the Rikers' sofa and having a little supper. Safe topics would be: the weather, the accident at the curling club, the teaser ads that had been running in the *Something,* Kip Mc-Diarmid's haiku that convulsed the literary club, and Yum Yum's hoarding of socks under the rya rug. There would also be

comment on Friday's alarming headline:

P.O. MURALS . . . MUST . . . GO!

The historic Moose County murals
that have made the Pickax post office
a tourist attraction and a mecca for the
citizenry are doomed to disappear.
Otherwise the building will be con-
demned as a public-safety hazard and
permanently closed.

Postmaster Bill Buncomb said, "This
comes as a shock! We were worried
about peeling paint drifting down on
customers like dandruff, but had no
idea it was life-threatening. But when
the experts tested it, they lowered the
boom."

The building will be closed until further notice, and post office business
will be shifted to the vacant buildings
on Book Alley.

County historian Homer Tibbitt said,
"When the murals were painted during
the Depression, there were no artists
here capable of working in heroic
scale, so artists were brought in from

elsewhere in the state, but they used local folks for models—miners, loggers, farmwives, and so on. Today their descendants come into the post office and see Grandma or Great-grandpa up there on the wall. She's pedaling a spinning wheel, and he's climbing up a ladder with coal dust on his face. It's a shame to take this away from them, but if the murals are life-threatening, there's no choice."

It was twilight when Qwilleran called for Polly, to go to see the Rikers' new sofa. Hearing no music as he passed Wetherby Goode's unit, he assumed his neighbor was in Horseradish with his inamorata. Kirt Nightingale's place was dark; he was undoubtedly at the country club. Polly was feeding the cats, and he helped by changing their drinking water and policing their commode. Then they strolled to The Birches.

Amanda's unit was dark; she might be dining with clients in Purple Point, who would be plotting her political career: first, mayor; then, county commissioner; then—?

Jeffa was home, and Robyn's car was there; there was a small robin painted on the driver's door.

Susan's place was dark. Her bridge club would be meeting at the clubhouse and having a catered dinner. Some kind of chicken.

At the Rikers' condo the foursome assembled with the warm pleasure of old friends who see each other often. There were cries of, "Where's the sofa?"

It was admired from all angles, sat upon, and compared to the old one. The fabric, Mildred said, was an abstract jacquard weave treated to resist soil. The color, Arch said, was the color of good Scotch.

With Mildred's casserole of moussaka, Arch was serving a local wine from the Windy Cliff Vineyard in Brrr Township. For Qwilleran he had a white grapejuice imported from Ohio. He kept waving his hand over the top of the open bottles. "Fruit flies," he explained.

"In November?" Qwilleran asked.

Arch clapped his hands smartly together. "Got him!"

He looked at his palms. "The little devil got away!"

Mildred said, "They're not fruit flies, Arch. I'm afraid you have floaters."

"What? What?"

"Do you mean you reached middle-age without seeing small specks dancing in front of your eyes?"

"According to my ophthalmologist," Polly said, "the vitreous gel in the eye thickens or shrinks, forming clumps or strands that throw shadows on the retina."

"Frankly," Arch said, "I'd rather have fruit flies."

Qwilleran proposed a toast: "May you never be judged by the company you keep!" Then he entertained them with a story about Burgess Campbell's guide dog:

"Eddington Smith used to search for out-of-print titles for Burgess, and Alexander developed a platonic romance with Edd's cat. Winston would sit on the top step of the ladder, and meaningful glances would be exchanged between the two animals. After the disaster it seemed like the end of a beautiful friendship. . . . until Winston went to live with the Bethunes, next door to the Campbells! And now they commune silently between the side windows."

"Isn't that touching!" Mildred cried.

"Any excitement at the paper?" Qwilleran asked.

Arch said, "Our phones rang nonstop yesterday after the paper came out. Readers were mad as hornets about the post office story, as if it were our doing. People always want to shoot the messenger who brings bad news."

"The headline was . . . rather brutal," Polly said. "If the news could have been broken more gently . . . The quote from Homer Tibbitt was a good idea. Do you know he's in the hospital?"

"Oh, dear! At his age? It doesn't sound good."

"It's not as bad as you think," Polly said. "He's having a knee replacement in the Joint Replacement Spa on the top floor. They don't treat patients as if they're sick. It's like taking your car in for a brake relining. I phoned Rhoda, and she said he's having a wonderful time. He's not stuck in a hospital room, in a hospital gown. The patients get together in a large pleasant room, and family members can visit them there."

"Then I don't have to send him a cheer-up card," Arch said. "He can send *me* a cheer-up card."

Everyone was relaxed. Conversation flowed easily. Dessert was a chocolate sundae with a topping of pistachio nuts.

The party ended early, and Polly invited Qwilleran in for music.

When he finally returned to Unit Four, the Siamese were waiting politely for their tuck-in ritual. . . . but the living room was a mess. Koko had been on a paper-shredding binge and had reduced the *Something* to ticker tape and confetti. That smart cat had discovered that newsprint tears more successfully lengthwise than crosswise! What was on his mind? He had oblique ways of communicating. He might be suggesting that he preferred torn paper in his commode—and not the expensive dustproof, scatterproof litter. Or was he editorializing on the post office story, the haiku, or the big teaser ad promising fun for the whole family? What kind of fun?

*   *   *

The next afternoon all was quiet in Unit Four. Qwilleran was reading, and the Siamese were catnapping, when Koko suddenly bolted out of his lethargy as if shot and started racing around the house: over tables, around the kitchen, up the stairs, down to the living room sofa like a flying squirrel, toppling a lamp, scattering everything else.

It was a first-class catfit. The Big One's coming, Qwilleran thought.

The insane chase ended on the fireplace mantel, where Koko stood on his hind legs and pawed the batik—pawed the red patches of dye that were robins.

Something twitched on Qwilleran's upper lip, and something clicked in his brain. He phoned Unit Two at The Birches. "Susan, is there such a thing as an emergency manicure?"

"No, darling. Are your fingernails falling off? Robyn is right next door with Jeffa. Shall I send her over?"

"I'll be much in your debt, Susan."

"How about selling me the martini pitcher?"

"Not *that* much in your debt."

In a few minutes the manicurist arrived with her businesslike black kit. "Susan says you have a problem, Mr. Q."

"Yes. It's very good of you to come on short notice."

"Where shall we work? At the kitchen table?"

Sitting across from her, he first grasped her hands and said with sincerity, "Before we begin, let me extend my deep sympathy to you and Mrs. Young."

She lowered her eyes. "Thank you. I feel so sorry for Jeffa—losing her husband, moving to a strange town to be with her son, then losing him so tragically."

They observed a moment of respectful silence. Then she said, "You have spatulate fingers, Mr. Q. They make a strong hand for a man."

In a flashback he recalled acting in college plays and gloating over critics' praise of his "strong gestures." Was it only a matter of spatulate fingers?

"Now what's the problem, Mr. Q?"

"My problem, Robyn, is in accepting Cass's death as an accident. I feel strongly about it."

She looked up hopefully. "I do, too! I don't know what to do."

"Did he have enemies?"

"Well . . . Don blamed Cass for breaking up our marriage, but it was doomed long before I met Cass."

"How did you meet him?"

"Well . . . XYZ executive meetings were held at our house, and I was supposed to serve the drinks and then disappear, but Cass liked to talk to me about nature and the environment. I love the outdoors. . . . After what happened at Breakfast Island, Cass and Doctor Zoller disagreed with Don a lot. I knew about their fights because the walls of these condos are thin. They had a violent argument over the payday loan company that Don wanted XYZ to start. Don said it was legal, and he could get a permit. Dr. Zoller said it was unethical and immoral, it exploited working people. That's when he and Cass resigned."

"Who are Don's new associates? Do you know?"

"No. I'd checked out by then. But strange things are happening. The doctor told Cass they should both get out of town while they were still healthy. Cass didn't take him seriously."

"Before you leave," he said, "look at the wall hanging over the fireplace."

"Robins!" she cried. She pulled up a pantleg to show a small robin tattoo on her ankle. "An artist in Bixby does butterflies, squirrels, anything you want. It's a permanent symbol of your commitment to the environment. As soon as I filed for divorce, I got this tattoo and dyed my hair the reddest red there is! I'll give you the artist's number, if you're interested."

She left, and the Siamese jumped down from the refrigerator. They had been listening, concerned about what she was doing to him.

Qwilleran hoped Polly was not looking out the window when the striking redhead walked past. He hoped she was still putting away summer cottons and getting out winter tweeds. If she saw Robyn, she would not recognize her as the colorless Mrs. Exbridge.

Polly would ask, "Who was that striking redhead?" If he said, "My manicurist," she would not believe it. He would say, "She was collecting for homeless cats and dogs, and when you didn't answer your doorbell, I gave her a generous donation in your name." *That* she would believe.

seventeen

Koko was a cat of many interests—
most of them short-lived, all of them
intense. Now it was the glove box! Earlier
he had spent hours investigating the high-
lights and shadows within the crystal martini pitcher. He had played fast and loose
with a bowl of wooden apples, as if point-
ing out that they were not the real thing:
that cat knew right from wrong. He had
rubbed his jaw on the sharp corners of the
pyramid lampshade tilting it or twisting it.
Why? Only a cat would know. . . . Now
his obsession was the glove box.

"What's going on with you and that box,
young man?" Qwilleran asked, and Koko

squeezed his eyes. He could contract his long, sleek body into a pouf of fur to fit the five-by-fourteen surface exactly, looking like an Egyptian sphinx from the book on the coffee table. Sometimes he exercised his footpads on the carving or sniffed the hinges or pawed the latch.

"There's nothing inside but gloves!" Qwilleran told him. Then he thought, We're not connecting. . . . What does he want? . . . He's trying to tell me something. . . . Does he want to get into the box?

Qwilleran was well aware that cats like to hide in boxes, wastebaskets, drawers, cabinets, bookcases, closets, and stereo systems—not to mention abandoned refrigerators and packing cases about to be shipped to Omaha.

"Okay, have it your way, you rascal!" He lifted the cat unceremoniously from his perch, opened the lid, and removed three pairs of winter gloves. "It's all yours!"

It was a heavy box, the boards being oak and an inch thick. The lid tilted back on its hinges like a shelf. Koko approached cautiously, first studying the interior, then sniffing the surfaces, corners, and joinings. One would be led to wonder what esoteric secrets, or priceless treasures, or illegal substances had been stored there.

Qwilleran himself could detect nothing. "Enough of this nonsense! . . . Treat!"

It was the magic word. Yum Yum suddenly appeared from one of the lairs where she made herself invisible; Koko strolled nonchalantly to the feeding station. And that was the end of the glove box. . . . That is, until the next morning.

After Koko had finished his breakfast, he walked directly to the glove box as if it were his assignment for the day. It was still open, and he jumped in, settling down in a huddled posture to fit the space: back humped, head and ears alert, tail drooping over the outside of the box.

It was obvious to Qwilleran that the cat's body seemed elevated as if on a cushion. He brought a ruler from his desk and measured the height of the box and the depth of the interior. It was six inches outside, four inches inside.

"A false bottom!" he said aloud. "Sorry to disturb you, old boy."

He closed the lid and turned the box over for examination. As he did so, there was an unexpected sound from within—not a rattle but a *swish.* He grasped the box firmly and shook it hard. Something was sliding about inside: an old love letter? A deed to the old homestead? A forgotten stock certificate now worth millions? Whatever it was, Koko had known that something was entombed. It might be the skeleton of a mouse or the turnkey from a sardine can. Chuckling, Qwilleran tackled the secret compartment—pressing, prying, pounding while Koko yowled at his elbow. The more vigorous the attack, the more active the contents and the louder the yowls. Attracted by the excitement, Yum Yum was adding her shrieks.

"Shut up!" the man yelled, and the cats turned up the volume.

Qwilleran had an urge to take a hatchet to the stubborn chunk of wood but was saved by the telephone bell.

"Good morning, dear," said Polly. "I'll be chained to my desk all day and would appreciate some oranges and pears, if you're coming in to Toodle's."

He agreed and at the same time solved his own problem. Susan Exbridge had a desk in her shop with a secret compartment; she would have a suggestion. The box he would leave at home, however. He was not supposed to have it. Polly would not want it known that she had given away Kirt's heirloom, and Susan would be too curious about what came out of it.

Her store hours were eleven-maybe to five-maybe. He dressed and drove downtown at eleven. Of course, she was not there. He stood on the street corner trying to decide where to go for coffee.

The center of town seemed unusually crowded. It looked as if a parade were scheduled. There were two PPD patrol cars in evidence. Qwilleran went to investigate.

Three officers were milling around, and one of them was Andrew Brodie; it had to be important to bring the chief out. Pedestrians were spilling out into the street, and police were detouring southbound traffic through Book Alley. One lane was kept open for northbound. Qwilleran quickened his pace when he realized the crowd was surging around the post office. They were noisy but not belligerent.

"What's up, Andy?" he called out.

"Protest about the murals. Peaceful so far."

There were no picket signs, no photographers, no officials to hear the complaints—just townfolk feeling bad and saying, "Isn't it terrible?"

The chief said, "We need to bring it to a head, Qwill, so they'll go home and let traffic get back to normal—before some hothead throws a brick. . . . Why don't you go up there and talk to them?"

"Me?"

"You've got the gift of gab, and they'll listen to you." Without further words, Brodie grabbed his arm and started hustling him through the crowd. "Coming through! Make way! Step back, please!"

Onlookers recognized the moustache. "Is that *him?* . . . It's Mr. Q! . . . Is he gonna talk to us?"

A flight of four steps on one side, and a ramp on the other, led to the post office doors. Qwilleran mounted the steps to the small concrete stoop and turned to face the assemblage. The babble of voices became a tumult of cheers and applause, until he raised his hand for silence.

Before he could speak, a man's voice called out, "Where's Koko?"

There was a burst of laughter.

Koko's amusing and exasperating antics were chronicled in the "Qwill Pen," reminding readers of their own unpredictable felines.

Qwilleran, speaking with his theatre voice that required no microphone or bullhorn, said that Koko was at home, devising something special in the way of a catfit to usher in the Big One.

The tension was broken. He surveyed his audience with the brooding gaze that they always construed as sympathetic. "I know why you're here, and I know how you feel. I feel the same way. Most of you have had a lifelong friendship with these murals. You know the nineteenth-century pioneers as if they were your neighbors. You can see them with your eyes closed: tilling a field with a horse-drawn plow, spinning wool on a wheel, building a log cabin, shoeing a horse, riding a log run down the river, drying fishnets on the beach, carrying a pickax and a lunch bucket to the mine. And you know what he's got for lunch."

"A pasty!" everyone shouted.

"But time changes all things. The colors are fading, and the paint is flaking—a serious health hazard. Do we want to board up the murals and paint the walls government tan?"

"No! No!"

"Then let's commission a new generation of artists to depict pioneer life with understanding and historic accuracy. It's the kind of people-friendly project that the K Fund believes in—"

Cheers interrupted, and Qwilleran took the opportunity to mop his brow.

"The art studio that painted Moose County landscapes on the bookmobile would find it a challenge to depict primitive landscapes and early settlers with their ox-carts and sailing ships and log cabins. The original murals are being professionally photographed for the historic record and for the guidance of artists who will replicate them. . . . and in a memorial booklet available without charge to every family in Pickax."

A news photographer appeared. Qwilleran was mobbed by enthusiasts. Here was the "Qwill Pen" in the flesh—Koko's godparent—Santa Claus without a beard. Eventually Brodie extricated him and drove him to the antique shop. "Who tipped off the photographer?" Qwilleran asked.

"The paper picked it up from the police radio," said the chief. "All that guff you gave them—was that the honest truth?"

"You shoved me in front of them. I had to make up something," Qwilleran said.

"Got any coffee?" Qwilleran grumbled as he barged into Susan's shop.

"Darling! What happened? You look . . . frazzled!"

"Skip the compliments. Just pour the coffee."

She led him back to her office. "What on earth have you been doing?"

"You'll read about it in the paper. And in case you're wondering where your customers are, they're all down at the post office. But they'll be here in a few minutes. Meanwhile, I'd like a hostess gift for Mildred Riker. We had dinner there the other night. You were out, whooping it up."

Susan rolled her eyes. "A customer invited me to a birthday party at the country club, and I had to go because she'd just made a huge purchase. I sat next to the mayor, and I thought it was rather gauche of him to try to sell me some investments between the soup course and the entrée."

280 LILIAN JACKSON BRAUN

"What kind of investments?"

"A special package that pays enormous interest. He had the nerve to give me his card, so I gave him my card and said I buy family heirlooms."

"Good for you! Now what do you recommend for Mildred?"

"She'd like a bone china teacup and saucer for her collection. I keep them in stock. They're not old, but collectors come in to buy one and see a Duncan Phyfe table they can't live without, or an original Tiffany lamp."

"You're a crafty one, Susan," he said, "but you'll never sell a Duncan Phyfe *anything* to me!"

"I know, darling, but I love you in spite of it. It's your moustache! So cavalier! When Polly gets tired of you, I'll be waiting in the wings. . . . Now about Mildred's teacup," she went on in her businesslike way. "She collects the rose pattern, and I think the yellow rose would be good. Want me to giftwrap it and drop it off at her place on my way home? What do you want on the card?"

* * *

Qwilleran was halfway home before realizing he had forgotten his prime mission: fruit for Polly and information on false bottoms. Oh, well . . .

The Siamese met him with a loud two-part reminder that it was half past treat time. Absently he poured out a dish of crunchies while pondering the mystery of the glove box. Once more he made an attack on the top, bottom, sides, inside, and outside—without a clue.

Then, from the kitchen came a familiar but regrettable sound. One of the cats was "sleigh-riding" or "bottom-sliding" as it was sometimes called. Qwilleran shrugged and said aloud, "Cats will be cats!"

Without stopping to figure the connection, his mind flashed to another wooden box in his life—when he was growing up. It held dominoes. It had a sliding lid, virtually invisible unless one knew about it. The glove box might have a sliding bottom!

Grasping it in both hands and pushing hard with both thumbs, he held his breath. Nothing happened. Turning the box around he pushed from the other end. Ah! A faint crack appeared! It was a tight fit, but gradually the gap opened to a few inches. He could see an envelope inside and could even pull it out without struggling further.

It was addressed to one Helen Omblower in Chipmunk, and the sender was G. Omblower in Pennsylvania; the return address was cryptic. It had been mailed twenty years before, and the envelope was yellow with age. Both Koko and Yum Yum found it highly sniff-worthy. The enclosed note was equally cryptic. What interested Qwilleran was the unusual name. He looked it up in the phone book, but it was not listed. He would ask the Tibbitts; they knew everyone. Where had Kirt's mother found the box? In a secondhand shop? It was a handsome piece of carving. Had she tried to open it to retrieve the letter?

His ruminations were interrupted by a phone call from Polly, exclaiming, "My hero!"

"What do you mean?" he asked. "I forgot your pears and oranges."

"They weren't all that important. It was your performance in front of the post office that mattered!"

"Somebody had to say something."

"Don't be modest. You saved the day! Everyone who walked into the library today was raving about your speech! You stole the show from the Big One! Do you know the Last Drink flags are going up all over the county? The Village party will be held tonight—at the clubhouse as usual—Open House from five till midnight, with cash bar, snacks, informal entertainment, and card games. It's very casual. Just drop in."

Qwilleran said, "We could have dinner at the Nutcracker Inn first. It may close after snow flies. And I want to visit Homer before the Big One."

He tracked down Rhoda Tibbitt at the Friendship Inn on the medical campus. "How is your indomitable spouse?"

"Just fine, Qwill. He's in the Joint Replacement Spa and having the time of his life, telling stories and keeping the other patients in stitches! They've given themselves nicknames. One old gentleman said, 'If you can be Homer, I want to be Chaucer.' And that started it. One woman wanted to be Emily Dickinson, and so forth."

"Do they welcome visitors?"

"By all means! Come before snow flies."

"As longtime residents of Moose County,

Rhoda, have you ever known anyone by the name of Helen Omblower? She lived in Chipmunk twenty years ago. That's all I know.''

There was a thoughtful pause. "It's ringing a distant bell. I'll ask Homer."

"You do that, and I'll see you both tomorrow."

eighteen

Tuesday was a sunny day with blue sky and puffy, white clouds, yet it was the official countdown before the Big One, and all Moose County was in a frenzy of stocking up on . . . everything. Qwilleran had asked the drugstore to save him a Sunday *New York Times,* which would keep him busy during the three-day blizzard. As he approached the store he recognized two men standing on the sidewalk. Ernie Kemple's booming voice said, "The shafthouse!" Then Burgess Campbell said something, and they both roared with laughter.

"What's the dirt, you guys?" Qwilleran

asked. "And why isn't Alexander laughing?"

Campbell's guide dog had the unflinching stoicism of his profession.

Kemple became suddenly serious. "Remember I wanted to put an antique mall in Otto's old building, Qwill? I've just found out what's going in there—the 'recreation center' that's been advertised in a teaser campaign. It's going to be a video palace with gambling machines on the balcony, and they're calling it The Shafthouse!"

"Because you'll get the shaft!" Burgess said.

They roared again.

"Why are we laughing?" said Ernie. "It's bad news!"

"How did you find out about this?" Qwilleran asked. "It's been the biggest secret since Hannibal crossed the Alps."

"My next-door neighbor has the trucking firm that delivered the equipment. The gambling machines go on the balcony."

"Wait a minute. I didn't know gambling was permitted in this town."

"Only if you get a special permit from the city council. Previous requests have been denied, but this time somebody had the right connections or greased the right palms."

Burgess said, "Alexander himself could get a license to sell booze in this town if he knew the right boots to lick."

When Qwilleran left with his armful of newspaper, he thought, This whole concept, including the name, is too sophisticated for the simple purveyor of "tasty eats." Is Otto one of the Donex associates? Is the mayor another? Is this one of the schemes that Zoller disapproved of? Is this one of the reasons he left town suddenly? It takes a special kind of courage to expose corruption in a small town.

It's easier and safer to move away.

The prospect of visiting a hospitalized ninety-eight-year-old is not usually a joyous one, but there was never anything usual about Homer Tibbitt, and Qwilleran looked forward to it. The lobby of Pickax General was aflutter with "canaries," the helpful volunteers in yellow smocks. One of them conducted Qwilleran to the Joint Replacement Spa on the top floor.

In an atrium under a skylight (not the real thing but psychologically effective) patients were lounging in specially designed furniture and indulging in spurts of laughter. Rhoda made the introductions: Chaucer, Pocahontas, Mark Twain, Paul Revere, Joan of Arc . . . "And this is our beloved Mr. Q!"

The response was instantaneous: "Love your column!" "How's Koko?" "My daughter won one of your pencils!" "Got your recumbent bike put away in mothballs?"

He replied, "I'm overwhelmed in the presence of so many world-renowned personages. It could only happen in Pickax. Where's Emily Dickinson?"

"Went home this morning. When she hears you were here, she'll be fit to be tied!"

"Who was telling bawdy jokes when I came in?" Qwilleran asked.

"We were playing think-games," Homer said. "We're making a collection of nostalgic sounds that you never hear anymore— or hardly ever. . . . Chaucer, do your impersonation of an old car with a weak battery, trying to start on a cold morning."

"I remember it well," the man said. "All over the neighborhood you'd hear *rrrgh rrrgh rrrgh* and then a pause. . . . *rrrgh*

rrrgh rrrgh rrrgh. The temperature was below zero, and the driver was sweating behind the wheel. Again *rrrgh rrrgh rrrgh rrrgh CHUG!* Hopeful silence. Then *rrrgh rrrgh rrrgh CHUG CHUG CHUG!* And the car roared down the street at fifteen miles an hour!"

There were others:

Laundry being scrubbed on a wooden washboard.

An officeful of manual typewriters all clattering at the same time.

A street urchin shouting, "Shoeshines for a nickel!"

The Sunday afternoon sound of cutting grass with a push-and-grunt lawnmower.

A windup gramophone running down in the middle of a record.

Then Rhoda explained that Mr. Q had come to discuss business with Homer, and the three of them retired to the privacy of a hospital room.

Homer said, "We've been cudgeling our brains about the Omblower name. Twenty years ago Rhoda was still teaching; I was retired as principal but still poking my nose into everything."

"Yes, and I remember a Mrs. Omblower," she said. "It was my year to do parent-liaison, and she was a pathetic little creature—single mother struggling to support herself and her son. She did house-cleaning, but it was difficult without a car. And her son got into trouble at school. He was a bright boy—an all-A student—but he had a lawbreaking streak."

"What laws did he break?" Qwilleran asked.

"Thou shalt not do homework for other students. . . . or sign parents' names to report cards . . . or write false absence excuses."

"Assuming he did it for money," Qwilleran said, "was he helping out at home?"

"That gives it a hint of nobility," Homer said, "but he was part of a white-collar crime ring—with two accomplices from affluent families. They were all smart kids who could have used their intelligence for leadership and creative purposes. They were just three bad apples in a barrel of good ones. That happens, you know."

Qwilleran's moustache bristled, and he fingered the letter in his pocket. "What measures did the school take?"

"The two students from good families

were privately reprimanded and allowed to finish their senior year. Omblower dropped out."

"It was the kind of thing that the school suppressed," said Rhoda.

Qwilleran said, "Was his name George? I found a letter he wrote to his mother in Chipmunk twenty years ago. The return address on the envelope looks like that of a state prison." He read it to them.

Hi, Mom!

Just a note to let you know I'll be out soon, but if Denise is still around, tell her I'm dead. I'm getting a new identity—new occupation, new lifestyle, new everything!

I've learned a lot in five years. The trick is to live by your wits and not by the rules. So don't waste any prayers on me, Mom. I'll always be your bad apple.

George

Qwilleran said, "The handwriting is good, with a back-slant that's quite distinctive, and my proofreader's eye notes perfect spelling and punctuation."

There were murmured comments—from two listeners who knew not quite what to say.

Qwilleran asked, "Who were the affluent families? How did they get their wealth?"

"One from railroading, one from bootlegging," Homer said, adding quickly, "You're not going to write about this, are you?"

His wife said, "Homer, Qwill wouldn't waste his talent on muckraking."

Thinking fast, Qwilleran said, "I've found an old wood carving that would have sentimental value for Mrs. Omblower, if I could find her. I thought her son's two confederates might know her whereabouts."

Rhoda jumped up, consulting her watch. "Homer, it's time for your therapy. Sorry, Qwill. Would you excuse us? I'll walk you to the elevator." As soon as they were out of her husband's hearing, she said, "I don't want him to have a stroke. His blood pressure erupts when anyone mentions Gideon Blake. He's the 'bad apple' who earned two college degrees and returned under the name of Gregory Blythe. When Homer retired, the man became principal, wriggled out of a scandal, was elected mayor three times—oh! It's all too much for Homer!"

"I understand," Qwilleran said. "Take good care of our civic treasure!"

On the way to his van in the parking lot, Qwilleran came face to face with a large fierce-looking Scot in kilt and bonnet, with a bagpipe under his arm—a rare sight approaching a hospital building.

"Andy! What are you doing here?" he demanded.

"My old uncle is in there," the police chief said gloomily. "His dying wish is to hear the bagpipe once more. Sad business! When I've finished I'll be ready for a swig of the good stuff."

"I have a bottle of very good stuff," said Qwilleran, "if you don't mind driving out to Indian Village."

"I'll do that, but it'll be late—after ten. I take my wife out to dinner on my day off."

Qwilleran drove home with a happy foot on the pedal. He had missed his confabs with the chief—exchanging suspicions, private theories, and sometimes inside information.

At home he was met by a highly nervous Yum Yum. She frisked about, not in anticipation of a treat but in disapproval of a misdemeanor.

"What's bugging you, sweetheart?" he asked, trying to pick her up for comforting, but she darted away and ran to the coffee table. There he found that a cat had up-chucked on his book about Egypt with its fine jacket illustration of pyramids in the desert. Fortunately the cover was pro-tected by a heavy polyurethane slipjacket. Even so, why had the cat elected that par-ticular spot for an indiscretion?

Obviously Koko was the culprit. Cats never covered for each other. The innocent one always circled and sniffed the scene of the crime. And where was the perpetrator? He was not hiding in guilt or shame or em-barrassment; he was sitting complacently on his cushion atop the refrigerator.

Silently Qwilleran did what had to be done. There was nothing to be gained by scolding. Perhaps Koko had an upset stomach, but he could have selected a more appropriate target.

Qwilleran stayed calm. And Koko was certainly calm. Only sweet little Yum Yum with her housekeeperly instincts suffered the stigma of it all. Qwilleran picked her up and carried her around the room several times, kneading her fur and murmuring in her ear—until she purred.

And as he walked, he pondered the remarkable creature named Kao K'o Kung, trying to communicate and failing to get through. . . . No wonder he tossed his cookies! And on my best book! What does he want to tell me?

A moment later Qwilleran had a brilliant idea. Putting Yum Yum down—gently—he phoned Kirt Nightingale and left a message on the machine.

"Kirt, this is Qwilleran. I've decided to go whole hog—David Roberts—Napoleon—and anything else you consider a wise investment. Could you come over tomorrow, about noon, and have a Bloody Mary and give me some advice? Just call and leave a yes or no on my machine."

When Qwilleran picked up Polly for a dinner date at the Nutcracker Inn, he was met at the door by Brutus, her self-appointed security officer, who accepted a small bribe. "The way to have a friend is to be a friend," said Qwilleran, "and that goes double for cats."

On the way to Black Creek he announced, "I've solved my Christmas-shopping problem!"

"I wish I could," she said. "What are you doing?"

"Giving everyone a gift certificate for an ankle tattoo at a Bixby art studio. It's now socially correct to declare your commitment to the environment by having a nature symbol tattooed on your ankle."

Her peals of laughter jolted his grip on the wheel. "Who gave you that idea?"

"You could have a butterfly or a mouse or a cardinal—"

"Cardinals are overdone. You see them on greeting cards, T-shirts, pot holders, wastebaskets—everywhere," she objected.

"You have plenty of time to decide. I visualize Arch with a bullfrog and Mildred with a white rabbit."

His manner was so serious, she never knew when she was being teased.

She said, "I saw Derek driving into our street the other day. I wonder what that was all about?"

"He and Wetherby were probably planning the entertainment for the party. I wouldn't be surprised if they did a tap dance."

Polly had never seen the tall brick mansion that housed the Nutcracker Inn.

"Wait till you see the interior," he said. "Fran Brodie was commissioned to furnish it in Stickley, like the Mackintosh Inn."

"But the atmosphere is different," she said as she entered. "Lighter and airier and friendlier. It's the pale coral walls!"

When the innkeeper welcomed them, he said to Qwilleran, "The young couple you recommended as innkeepers came in and introduced themselves. They have good personalities and credentials, and I told them—"

"Mr. Knox! Mr. Knox!" cried a young woman in a housekeeping smock as she rushed down the stairs from an upper floor. "Mrs. Smith on the third floor wants her dinner sent up on a tray."

"No problem," he said quietly. "Give the information to the hostess. And Cathy— walk, don't rush." To the guests he explained, "An MCCC student. Her first day on the job."

Polly said, "How well I remember my first day on my first job."

"Don't we all!"

In the dining room the tablecloths were the same pale coral. They both ordered grilled salmon—to go with the tablecloths, they said. Qwilleran grumbled that it must be the cook's first day on the job, too, although he finished every morsel on his plate.

Polly said, "Guess who came to the library today, bearing gifts? Misty Morghan! She's offering us two large batiks in splashy colors to brighten the reading room. I took her to lunch at Rennie's."

"What did you do with your trusty tuna sandwich?"

"Gave it to Mac and Katie. Misty claims to have a unique eye for hidden details, and she can tell when someone has had cosmetic surgery. She was glancing around the restaurant, and it struck me as invasion of privacy, but I reserved my opinion. She said to me, 'Don't look now, but the man over there has had a complete facial reconstruction.' He must have been in a devastating accident."

"Did you look?"

"Of course I looked! It was Kirt Nightingale! I always thought his expression was unemotional. I wonder if he's doing well with his catalogue."

Toward the end of the meal Qwilleran asked, "How do you feel about the Last Drink party?"

"Not strongly. How do you feel?"

"It's April fifteenth trying to be New Year's Eve, but we should make an appearance. I have to be home by ten; I'm expecting an important phone call."

When they left the dining room, the innkeeper asked if they had enjoyed their dinner, and they were trying to say something tactful, when the young housekeeper came bouncing down the stairs again.

"Mr. Knox! The lady on the third floor wants to know if Nicodemus could spend the night with her! She's lonesome for her five cats."

Hearing his name, a sleek black cat slinked into their midst—a cat with eyes that burned like live coals.

"Certainly," the innkeeper said. "Take him upstairs, and don't forget his water dish and commode."

Ah! Qwilleran thought. Maggie's still here!

nineteen

When Qwilleran and Polly arrived at the party, they were greeted effusively by their neighbors: "We were afraid you weren't coming! . . . Derek has written a new song. . . . What are you drinking? . . . Try some of the chicken liver pâté."

Wetherby Goode played a fanfare on the piano and announced, "And now the moment you have been waiting for! Derek Cuttlebrink plays his latest creation: 'Pickax the Proud'!"

There were cheers as everyone's favorite folksinger stepped to the microphone, strummed a few chords, and sang:

We're the friendly folk of Pickax,
*   U.S.A.*
We find each other's puppies when
*   they stray.*
*   Our bosses give us raises*
*   And we always sing their praises,*
And we're getting better-looking every
*   day.*

If someone does us dirt we never
*   sue.*
We lend the guy next door a buck or
*   two.*
*   We're the first at paying taxes*
*   And the last at grinding axes.*
And gossiping we never, never do!

When someone suggested making it the official anthem of Pickax City, the Villagers roared their approval. Derek winked broadly at Qwilleran, who left immediately with Polly—both of them murmuring excuses and regrets.

Around ten o'clock the Siamese were watching Qwilleran prepare a tray of beverages and cheeses when their heads swiveled toward the foyer. An unearthly sound was coming from the street.

On the sidewalk stood Andrew Brodie in the fatigues he usually wore to rake leaves, and he was piping a wild Scottish dance.

When the last bouncing, heel-clicking notes had trailed off into silence, Qwilleran called out, "Andy! What's that insane tune?"

"The Drunken Piper."

"Then come in and sober up."

He followed Qwilleran into the kitchen, dropping the bagpipe on the sofa. There the Siamese could sniff the strange animal and decide whether it was dead or alive.

"How did it go at the hospital?"

"I played his favorite hymns, and he was peaceful when I left."

The refreshments were served in the living room, where there was a small fire crackling in the grate. The guest looked about appreciatively. "Pretty big robins, those . . . are those apples real? . . . That pitcher is some chunk of glass!" Then he asked, "How come you aren't out having a Last Drink?"

"This is my Last Drink."

"Are you one of those idiots who rush

out into the street when snow starts to fly and stick out their tongues?"

"I can't say I fit that description."

"If a snowflake lands on your tongue, it's supposed to be good luck. Downtown will be full of crazy fools running around with tongues hanging out like overheated dogs."

The telephone rang. "Let it ring," Qwilleran said. "I think they'll leave a message."

After a few rings, a man's voice said, "Qwill, this is Kirt. The answer is yes. Tomorrow at twelve noon. You're making a wise choice."

"Are you ready for the Big One tonight?" Brodie asked.

"I don't expect it as soon as the National Weather Service predicts. When my weather cat stages his meteorological catfit, it'll be time to batten down the hatches."

"One of my neighbor's kids won a pencil in your contest. He wrote a poem about his cats. . . . Where are your chums?"

"The little pickpocket has an eye on your wristwatch. The smart one, as you call him, is staring at you from the stairs and wondering when the law agencies are going to solve a perfectly obvious case."

"What's his take on the situation?" Brodie asked as seriously as if consulting Hercule Poirot.

"First, let me refresh your drink," Qwilleran said, "and help yourself to the cheese." He took his time before answering the question. "If you've never heard Koko's death howl in the middle of the night, you don't know what cold sweat is all about. It means murder! He howled at the precise moment when Ruff Abbey was shot. . . . and again when Cass Young was killed. But first he howled when the thousands of books were burned. Koko considers that murder. . . . and by the way, arson was ruled out, but I have a theory about that."

"Let's hear it!"

"Some unauthorized individual let himself in the back door, and Edd's cat escaped, thus saving his life. Winston had never wanted to go out, but his animal instinct warned him of impending evil—the same instinct that charges Koko's batteries."

"Assuming that the three incidents are

three felonies, is Koko prepared to finger any suspects?"

"Yow!" came a comment from the stairs, as Koko heard his name.

"There's your answer," Qwilleran said. "Does the name Omblower mean anything to you?"

"Nope. Odd name."

"George Omblower was one of three bad boys at Pickax High School at one time, and I think he's back again—with an alias. . . . What do you know about the Donex Associates?"

Brodie harrumphed. "I'm not at liberty to talk, but there may be some interesting news in your paper tomorrow."

"Meanwhile, Omblower is coming here for a Bloody Mary at noon tomorrow, and I plan to ask him some embarrassing questions. Depending on how he reacts, a cop on the premises might be able to make an arrest."

"You serious?"

"Never more so! But the guy lives only two doors away, so we can't have any police vehicles at the curb."

"We can handle that," Brodie said.

* * *

The next morning Qwilleran phoned the concierge at the Pet Plaza. "Do you board cats by the hour?"

Lori Bamba had been his friend-in-need ever since he arrived in Moose County. "Not usually," she said, "but . . ."

"I need to get them off the premises for a few hours—for reasons too complicated to describe."

"When?"

"Now."

"We'll send our limousine over in half an hour. Your carrier or ours?"

Qwilleran lured the Siamese into the kitchen with a small treat, then stuffed them into their carrier. It was a loose fit for two sleek Siamese—unless they preferred not to travel. Then they puffed themselves up to resemble two porcupines on stilts.

"Consider this a mini-vacation at an exclusive resort," he said. "Behave like patricians." Two pairs of eyes glowered at him through the metal mesh of their prison.

Shortly after the limousine had whisked them away to the Pet Plaza, a plumber's van pulled up, and a man approached Unit Four with a kit of plumber's tools. "Got a leak?" he asked with a grin when Qwilleran opened the door.

"Come in, Pete," he said, recognizing a deputy from the sheriff's department.

Pete spoke a few words into his cell phone, and the plumbing van drove away. "What's up, Mr. Q?"

"A guy is coming here to sell me some books, and he happens to be a suspect in a murder case. I intend to ask him some leading questions—not about books—and you're here in case he gets nasty. The spare room on the balcony will be your observation post."

"We're supposed to tape the interrogation, so I'd better get set up."

"Feel free to move anything around if necessary, and let me know if there's anything you need."

The doorbell rang again. A pizza wagon stood at the curb, and a delivery man handed him a large, square, flat box. Qwilleran recognized him as an officer from the PPD.

"Hi, Mr. Q! Brodie sent this for your party. I hear it's gonna be fun and games today." He mumbled into his cell phone, and the pizza wagon took off.

* * *

As noon approached, the pizza was in the warming oven, the two officers were upstairs, and Qwilleran was at the bar, readying tomato juice, vodka, hot sauce, and a fresh lime. He was having second thoughts about trapping the quiet, sober-faced specialist in rare books. Just because the man had given Polly his mother's glove box, it was no proof that she was Helen Omblower. Kirt's mother might have bought the box at a local antique shop, never guessing that a letter was hidden in a false bottom. Neither did Polly, and Qwilleran himself had not discovered it until Koko commenced sniffing and pawing.

If Nightingale were indeed Omblower, as Qwilleran suspected, body language would reveal his guilt unless . . . he happened to be a skilled actor; acting might be one of the things he boasted of learning while in prison. (Don't wet lips; don't blink; don't scratch neck; don't pull earlobe.) Qwilleran began to wish Koko were there to contribute an occasional "Yow" and "Ik ik ik."

The doorbell rang, and the quiet, sober-faced bookseller stood there without uttering a sociable word, leaving it up to the host to say, "Good morning! Come in and have a *last* Last Drink."

In the foyer Nightingale glanced about warily, then walked to the sofa. "Interesting piece of glass," he said. "Does it have a pedigree?"

"St. Louis lead crystal, made for the French steamship lines. Weighs a ton."

"There's a fine book about glassmakers of the world if you're interested: Baccarat, Steuben, Waterford, Orrefors, and so forth—absolutely the definitive work."

"Right now I'm interested in Egypt," Qwilleran said. "But first drink to the Big One! We'll all be glad when snow flies and we can stop worrying about wildfires—or whatever they are. A lot of people think they're arson."

"Is that so?"

"Strange thing about arson: Property owners used to burn their buildings to collect insurance. Now arson is the most common type of vandalism. Structures are torched for thrills or just plain meanness. There's a rumor that a land-grabber burned the bookstore in order to get an affordable site in a good location—for sale to a commercial developer. . . . As a bookman, Kirt, you must have been horrified to see thousands of books go up in flames."

"There wasn't much of value there," said the bookman. "I spent several hours on the ladder and found nothing worthwhile."

"Be that as it may, it was the pride of Pickax, and Eddington himself was a leading citizen." Qwilleran stroked his moustache. "It hasn't been announced as yet, but I propose to establish a Rare Book Room at the public library, as a memorial to Eddington. That's why I asked you here today—to suggest acquisitions."

His guest bristled with interest.

"As a centerpiece, Kirt, I would like to suggest the three-volume set of David Roberts' lithographs. And while I refresh your drink, would you take this card and jot down other titles that a Rare Book Room should have on exhibit."

"A pleasure!" said Nightingale.

"With the K Fund behind it, cost should be no consideration. We'd like to think that tourists who used to head for the funny old bookstore will in the future head for the Eddington Smith Memorial and its fabulous books." Qwilleran suppressed a chuckle as he thought of the two officers on the balcony, taping the grandiose speech.

He took his time in mixing another Bloody Mary and cutting wedges of pizza for a snack, while Nightingale made his list with obvious relish.

When Qwilleran looked at this list, he nodded with satisfaction. It was written in the unique backhand of George Omblower.

Both men enjoyed the pizza, and Qwilleran explained that it came from a pizza parlor in Kennebeck that delivered. Food and drink and the prospect of a lucrative sale had apparently mellowed Nightingale's usual stiff formality.

It was time for Qwilleran to go to work. "You must have noticed many changes in Pickax, Kirt: medical center, airport, community college, curling club. I saw you there the other evening—the night Cass fell down the stairs. Are you a member?"

"I have a social membership, that's all. Friendly crowd."

"How long have you been gone from what we call God's country?"

"Perhaps twenty-five years. Time flies."

"I suppose you attended Pickax High School."

The guest nodded, dismissing it as a topic worth exploring.

"They have an Olympic-size swimming pool now."

"Is that so?"

"Did you by any chance know a student named George Omblower?" Qwilleran thought he detected a slight wince.

"Can't say that I did."

"He was an all-A student and considered quite a brain. Unfortunately he got into trouble and dropped out. A friend of mine knew his mother. She lived in Chipmunk. George had a girlfriend here who moped over him for years and then finally jumped off the Bloody Creek bridge." This was a fictional touch of Qwilleran's, but it stirred no emotion in his listener. "Mrs. Omblower said her son ran afoul of the law in the East and spent five years in prison."

Although Nightingale did not wet his lips or pull his earlobe, a flush came to his neck.

"There was another notoriously bad boy at the high school, named . . ." Qwilleran looked at the ceiling as if trying to recall the name, and he saw the guest room door open slowly and noiselessly. "I believe the name was Gideon Blake."

"No recollection. Is there a point to all this?" The man's temper was rising.

"Gideon got in trouble, too, but changed his name and became mayor of our fair city."

Nightingale took a gulp of his Bloody Mary.

"The only reason I'm boring you with this local gossip is to acquaint you with a rumor that Omblower is back in town under an alias and is wanted on charges of arson and murder."

Nightingale, clearly disturbed, set down his glass with a crash, and Qwilleran moved casually to the fireplace to stir the small blaze in the grate—and to get his hand on the poker. He turned just in time to see something flying in his direction. He dodged, and the missile sailed past his ear and crashed into the sliding glass door. At the same time there were thundering commands from the balcony and clattering boots on the stairs. Outside the shattered door, the martini pitcher landed unharmed on its solid bottom—on the cedar deck.

* * *

The vehicles that had moved quietly into River Road on a signal from the balcony now sped out of the Village with the suspect in the sheriff's car and the left-over pizza in the PPD car. Qwilleran, before calling the Pet Plaza, notified the maintenance crew to remove the broken glass and board up the sliding door.

When the Siamese arrived, they knew something monstrous had happened, even without visible evidence, and they were disinclined to leave the carrier. Only smoked oysters tempted them to return to the real world. Even so, they approached the treat with bellies to the floor and frequent glances over the shoulder.

Eventually Koko—but not timid Yum Yum—prowled about the scene of the crime. Amazingly, he first inspected the martini pitcher, now posed in the center of the coffee table as if nothing had happened. If the condo had been built according to code, with safety glass, it would have lost a handle.

"Any comment?" Qwilleran asked Koko. "You won't be quoted."

The cat was speechless.

The telephone rang, and it was Arch Riker's urgent voice.

"Have you heard the news? We have a bulletin on the front page. The mayor's been arrested."

"On what grounds?"

"Operating an illegal investment scheme, called a Ponzi scheme. . . . Amanda will be taking off her clothes and dancing in the street!"

"So will Homer Tibbitt."

"Amanda will win the election unopposed."

Qwilleran asked, "Exactly what is a Ponzi scheme?"

"Well, as I understand it," Arch said, "a broker takes a client's dough to invest in some promising business that needs cash to get started and will pay big interest. The deal sounds so good that the client's friends and relatives rush to invest their kids' college funds and retirement nest eggs. On paper it looks great. They give the broker more dough. . . . Of course, the crunch is that he never invested it—just used it for his own purposes. It's sometimes called pyramiding."

"Pyramiding!" Qwilleran repeated with a

look of wonderment. Was that why Koko was always twisting the brown lampshade. Or was he doing it because cats like to twist lampshades?

Qwilleran had a great desire to go downtown, mingle with the crowd, take the public pulse. Driving his van, he thought, Zoller blew the whistle. It takes a special kind of nerve to expose corruption in a small town. He took Maggie along under the guise of an elopement. He sent her back with the documents or whatever evidence he had. She lay low, delivering the papers to Zoller's attorney, who worked with the prosecutor.

Was it the barometric pressure of the approaching storm? Or was it relief at seeing a dubious character exposed? Hordes of people poured out into the downtown streets—some of them inebriated, all of them giddy with the news. The PPD was keeping an eye on them, although the officers were smiling as broadly as the celebrating citizens. In the post office, the bank, the stores—it was the same.

Qwilleran went to the police station, and Brodie waved him into his office. "What'd I tell ya? Have a cup of coffee."

"Well, you trapped the rat," Qwilleran said, "with all due respect to the mayoral office."

"And we're charging Nightingale with arson and murder. How did you get the idea he was Omblower?"

"Koko found the evidence. He also suspected Don Exbridge's letter in praise of shafthouses and the follow-up letters in opposition—not to mention the leader ads for the video palace."

"It would do me a lot of good to confiscate the gambling machines. Our people don't need those. Let them play bingo."

Qwilleran asked, "How about Don Exbridge? He's always working against the public good and getting away with it."

"He'll be accused as accomplice-before-the-fact, you can be sure. Everything was his idea. Omblower did the dirty work, and he won't let Exbridge go scot-free. . . . What was the crash I heard on the tape?"

"Nightingale picked up the martini pitcher by the handle and aimed it at my head like a hammer-throw. I ducked, and it sailed through Exbridge's cheap glass door, landing rightside-up on the soft cedar deck."

Brodie said, "A foolish man, Exbridge—using arson as a shortcut to acquiring land for development."

"No doubt about it, Andy: He wanted Book Alley for a strip mall downtown, and he wanted ten minesites for country estates and high-density condominiums."

Before leaving downtown Qwilleran visited the library to break the news to Polly. She already knew—through the grapevine.

"It's hard to believe," she said, "that Kirt would be involved like that. He seemed like a decent sort, and he loved books."

"He *sold* books," he corrected her.

As he drove to Indian Village, the sky became leaden, and dusk was falling early. He was not surprised to see the interior of Unit Four in a state of confusion. Everything that was not nailed down had been knocked to the floor—almost everything. Strangely, the martini pitcher, bowl of wooden apples and glove box were untouched. But Qwilleran's desktop was swept clean, two lamps were toppled, and the Danish rug was crumpled like an un-

made bed. This was a catfit at its worst—
or best, depending on one's point of view.

Koko was obviously pleased with his
performance. He lounged full-length on the
mantel and surveyed the clutter with satisfaction. And where was Yum Yum? Huddled in the spectator gallery on the stairs,
guarding a treasure that the police had left
behind: a stick of chewing gum, probably
the first she had ever seen.

Qwilleran had survived enough catfits to
know what to do: Stay calm; don't scold;
clean up.

As he worked, he considered the status
quo. The catfit marked the advent of the
Big One—but also the closure of the Three
Bad Apples case. He knew by experience
that Koko would now lose interest in apples, robins, carved boxes, and letters to
the editor. It proved one of two theories:
Either Koko was consciously exposing
evil . . . or he was just a cat, briefly interested in this or that, and the connections
were all coincidental. There were no abso-
lute answers. Scientists, having heard of
the cat's aptitudes through a police lieuten-
ant Down Below, had wanted to study
Koko's brain, but Qwilleran flatly refused.

He preferred to attribute Koko's gifts to his sixty whiskers.

For the cats' dinner Qwilleran diced turkey from Toodle's deli; for himself he opened a can of soup. Then he read aloud, with Yum Yum curled on his lap and Koko sitting tall on the arm of the chair. At one point, both small bodies tensed, and heads turned toward the front windows. Then both cats raced to the kitchen window. All was silent outdoors, and the night was dark, but light from the kitchen revealed the first few snowflakes fluttering lazily to the parched earth.

A deep gurgling sound came from Koko, and a faint mewing from Yum Yum. It was the prelude to the Big One!

Qwilleran grabbed his jacket and wool hat and went out the front door. The flakes meandered earthward like a gentle blessing. No neighbor was around to share the magical moment. Two delicate snowflakes came to rest on his moustache. And then— why not? He stuck out his tongue.